Three Frenchmen in Bengal

S.C. Hill

Contents

THREE FRENCHMEN
IN BENGAL

BY

S.C. Hill

TO

MY DEAR WIFE

PREFACE

This account of the commercial ruin of the French Settlements, taken almost entirely from hitherto unpublished documents, originated as follows. Whilst engaged in historical research connected with the Government Records in Calcutta, I found many references to the French in Bengal which interested me strongly in the personal side of their quarrel with the English, but the information obtainable from the Indian Records alone was still meagre and incomplete. A few months ago, however, I came across Law's Memoir in the British Museum; and, a little later, when visiting Paris to examine the French Archives, I found not only a copy of Law's Memoir, but also Renault's and Courtin's letters, of which there are, I believe, no copies in England. In these papers I thought that I had sufficient material to give something like an idea of Bengal as it appeared to the French when Clive arrived there. There is much bitterness in these old French accounts, and much misconception of the English, but they were written when misconception of national enemies was the rule and not the exception, and when the rights of non-belligerents were little respected in time of war. Some of the accusations I have checked by giving the English version, but I think that, whilst it is only justice to our Anglo-Indian heroes to let the world know what manner of men their opponents were, it is equally only justice to their opponents to allow them to give their own version of the story. This is my apology, if any one should think I allow them to say too much.

The translations are my own, and were made in a state of some perplexity as to how far I was bound to follow my originals--the writings of men who, of course, were not literary, and often had not only no pretension to style but also no knowledge of grammar. I have tried, however, to preserve both form and spirit; but if any reader is dissatisfied, and would like to see the original papers for himself, the courtesy of the Record officials in both Paris and London will give him access to an immense quantity of documents as interesting as they are important.

In the various accounts that I have used there are naturally slightly different versions of particular incidents, and often it is not easy to decide which is the correct one. Under the circumstances I may perhaps be excused for not always calling attention to discrepancies which the reader will detect for himself. He will also notice that the ground covered in one narrative is partly traversed in one or both of the others. This has been due to the necessity of treating the story from the point of view of each of the three chief actors.

I may here mention that the correspondence between Clive and the princes of Bengal, from which I have given some illustrative passages, was first seen by me in a collection of papers printed in 1893 in the Government of India Central Printing Office, Calcutta, under the direction of Mr. G.W. Forrest, C.I.E. These papers have not yet been published, but there exists a complete though slightly different copy of this correspondence in the India Office Library (Orme MSS. India XI.), and it is from the latter copy that I have, by permission, made the extracts here given. The remaining English quotations, when not from printed books, have been taken chiefly from other volumes of the Orme MSS., a smaller number from the Bengal and Madras Records in the India Office, and a few from MSS. in the British Museum or among the Clive papers at Walcot, to which last I was allowed access by the kindness of the Earl of Powis.

Finally, I wish to express my thanks to M. Omont of the Bibliotheque
Nationale, Paris, to Mr. W. Foster of the Record Department of the
India Office, and to Mr. J.A. Herbert of the British Museum, for
their kind and valuable assistance.

S.C. HILL.
September 6, 1903.

CHAPTER I
THE QUARREL WITH THE ENGLISH

Writing in 1725, the French naval commander, the Chevalier d'Albert, tells us that the three most handsome towns on the Ganges were Calcutta, Chandernagore, and Chinsurah, the chief Factories of the English, French, and Dutch. These towns were all situated within thirty miles of each other. Calcutta, the latest founded, was the greatest and the richest, owing partly to its situation, which permitted the largest ships of the time to anchor at its quays, and partly to the privilege enjoyed by the English merchants of trading freely as individuals through the length and breadth of the land. Native merchants and native artisans crowded to Calcutta, and the French and Dutch, less advantageously situated and hampered by restrictions of trade, had no chance of competing with the English on equal terms. The same was of course true of their minor establishments in the interior. All three nations had important Factories at Cossimbazar (in the neighbourhood of Murshidabad, the Capital of Bengal) and at Dacca, and minor Factories at Jugdea or Luckipore, and at Balasore. The French and Dutch had also Factories at Patna. Besides Calcutta, Chandernagore, and Chinsurah, the only Factory which was fortified was the English Factory at Cossimbazar.

During the long reign of the usurper, Aliverdi Khan,[1] that strong and politic ruler enforced peace among his European guests, and forbade any fortification of the Factories, except such as was

necessary to protect them against possible incursions of the
Marathas, who at that time made periodical attacks on Muhammadans
and Hindus alike to enforce the payment of the *chauth*,[2] or
blackmail, which they levied upon all the countries within their
reach. In Southern India the English and French had been constantly
at war whenever there was war in Europe, but in Bengal the strength
of the Government, the terror of the Marathas, and the general
weakness of the Europeans had contrived to enforce a neutrality.
Still there was nothing to guarantee its continuance if the fear of
the native Government and of the Marathas were once removed, and if
any one of the three nations happened to find itself much stronger
than the others. The fear of the Marathas had nearly disappeared,
but that of the Government still remained. However, it was not till
more than sixty years after the foundation of Calcutta that there
appeared any possibility of a breach of peace amongst the Europeans
in Bengal. During this time the three Factories, Calcutta always
leading, increased rapidly in wealth and importance. To the
Government they were already a cause of anxiety and an object of
greed. Even during the life of Aliverdi Khan there were many of his
counsellors who advised the reduction of the status of Europeans to
that of the Armenians, i.e. mere traders at the mercy of local
officials; but Aliverdi Khan, whether owing to the enfeeblement of
his energies by age or to an intelligent recognition of the value of
European commerce, would not allow any steps to be taken against the
Europeans. Many stories are told of the debates in his *Durbar*[3]
on this subject: according to one, he is reported to have compared
the Europeans to bees who produce honey when left in peace, but
furiously attack those who foolishly disturb them; according to
another he compared them to a fire[4] which had come out of the sea
and was playing harmlessly on the shore, but which would devastate
the whole land if any one were so imprudent as to anger it. His
wisdom died with him, and in April, 1756, his grandson,
Siraj-ud-daula, a young man of nineteen,[5] already notorious for

his debauchery and cruelty, came to the throne. The French--who, of all Europeans, knew him best, for he seems to have preferred them to all others--say his chief characteristics were cruelty, rapacity, and cowardice. In his public speeches he seemed to be ambitious of military fame. Calcutta was described to him as a strong fortress, full of wealth, which belonged largely to his native subjects, and inhabited by a race of foreigners who had grown insolent on their privileges. As a proof of this, it was pointed out that they had not presented him with the offerings which, according to Oriental custom, are the due of a sovereign on his accession. The only person who dared oppose the wishes of the young Nawab was his mother,[6] but her advice was of no avail, and her taunt that he, a soldier, was going to war upon mere traders, was equally inefficacious. The records of the time give no definite information as to the tortuous diplomacy which fanned the quarrel between him and the English, but it is sufficiently clear that the English refused to surrender the son of one of his uncle's *diwans*,[7] who, with his master's and his father's wealth, had betaken himself to Calcutta. Siraj-ud-daula, by the treacherous promises of his commanders, made himself master of the English Factory at Cossimbazar without firing a shot, and on the 20th of June, 1756, found himself in possession of Fort William, the fortified Factory of Calcutta.[8] The Governor, the commandant[9] of the troops, and some two hundred persons of lesser note, had deserted the Fort almost as soon as it was actually invested, and Holwell, one of the councillors, an ex-surgeon, and the gallant few who stood by him and continued the defence, were captured, and, to the number of 146, cast into a little dungeon,[10] intended for military offenders, from which, the next morning, only twenty-three came out alive. The English took refuge at Fulta, thirty miles down the river, where the Nawab, in his pride and ignorance, left them unmolested. There they were gradually reinforced from Madras, first by Major Kilpatrick, and later on by Colonel Clive and Admiral Watson. About the same time both French and English learned that war had been declared in Europe between England and France in the previous May, but, for different reasons, neither nation thought the time suitable for making the fact formally known.

Towards the end of December the English, animated by the desire of revenge and of repairing their ruined fortunes, advanced on Calcutta, and on the 2nd of January, 1757, the British flag again floated over Fort William. The Governor, Manik Chand, was, like many of the Nawab's servants, a Hindu. Some say he was scared away by a bullet through his turban; others, that he was roused from the enjoyment of a *nautch*--a native dance--by the news of the arrival of the English.[11] Hastening to Murshidabad, he reported his defeat, and asserted that the British they had now to deal with were very different from those they had driven from or captured in Calcutta.

The English were not satisfied with recovering Calcutta. They wished to impress the Nawab, and so they sent a small force to Hugli, which lies above Chandernagore and Chinsurah, stormed the Muhammadan fort, burnt the town, and destroyed the magazines, which would have supplied the Nawab's army in an attack on Calcutta. The inhabitants of the country had never known anything so terrible as the big guns of the ships, and the Nawab actually believed the men-of-war could ascend the river and bombard him in his palace at Murshidabad. Calling on the French and Dutch for aid, which they refused, he determined to try his fortune a second time at Calcutta. At first, everything seemed the same as on the former occasion: the native merchants and artisans disappeared from the town; but it was not as he thought, out of fear, but because the English wished to have them out of the way, and so expelled them. Except for the military camp to the north of the city, where Clive was stationed with his little army, the town lay open to his attack. Envoys from Calcutta soon

appeared asking for terms, and the Nawab pretended to be willing to
negotiate in order to gain time while he outflanked Clive and seized
the town. Seeing through this pretence Watson and Clive thought it
was time to give him a lesson, and, on the morning of the 5th of
February, in the midst of a dense fog, Clive beat up his quarters.
Though Clive had to retire when the whole army was roused, the
slaughter amongst the enemy had been immense; and though he
mockingly informed the Nawab that he had been careful to "injure
none but those who got in his way," the Nawab himself narrowly
escaped capture. The action, however, was in no sense decisive. Most
of the Nawab's military leaders were eager to avenge their disgrace,
but some of the chief nobles, notably his Hindu advisers,
exaggerated the loss already incurred and the future danger, and
advised him to make peace. In fact, the cruelty and folly of the
Nawab had turned his Court into a nest of traitors. With one or two
exceptions there was not a man of note upon whom he could rely, and
he had not the wit to distinguish the faithful from the unfaithful.
Accordingly he granted the English everything they asked for--the
full restoration of all their privileges, and restitution of all
they had lost in the sack of Calcutta. As the English valued their
losses at several hundreds of thousands, and the Nawab had found
only some L5000 in the treasury of Fort William, it is clear that
the wealth of Calcutta was either sunk in the Ganges or had fallen
as booty into the hands of the Moorish soldiers.

Siraj-ud-daula, though he did not yet know it, was a ruined man when
he returned to his capital. His only chance of safety lay in one of
two courses--either a loyal acceptance of the conditions imposed by
the English or a loyal alliance with the French against the English.
From the Dutch he could hope for nothing. They were as friendly to
the English as commercial rivals could be. They had always declared
they were mere traders and would not fight, and they kept their
word. After the capture of Calcutta the Nawab had exacted heavy

contributions from both the French and Dutch; but France and England were now at war, and he thought it might be possible that in these circumstances the restoration of their money to the French and the promise of future privileges might win them to his side. He could not, however, decide finally on either course, and the French were not eager to meet him. They detested his character, and they preferred, if the English would agree, to preserve the old neutrality and to trade in peace. Further, they had received no supplies of men or money for a long time; the fortifications of Chandernagore, i.e. of Fort d'Orleans, were practically in ruins, and the lesser Factories in the interior were helpless. Their military force, for attack, was next to nothing: all they could offer was wise counsel and brave leaders. They were loth to offer these to a man like the Nawab against Europeans, and he and his Court were as loth to accept them. Unluckily for the French, deserters from Chandernagore had served the Nawab's artillery when he took Calcutta, and it was even asserted that the French had supplied the Nawab with gunpowder; and so when the English heard of these new negotiations, they considered the proposals for a neutrality to be a mere blind; they forgot the kindness shown by the French to English refugees at Dacca, Cossimbazar, and Chandernagore, and determined that, as a permanent peace with the Nawab was out of the question, they would, whilst he hesitated as to his course of action, anticipate him by destroying the one element of force which, if added to his power, might have made him irresistible. They continued the negotiations for a neutrality on the Ganges only until they were reinforced by a body of 500 Europeans from Bombay, when they sent back the French envoys and exacted permission from the Nawab to attack Chandernagore. Clive marched on that town with a land force of 4000 Europeans and Sepoys, and Admiral Watson proceeded up the river with a small but powerful squadron.

Thus began the ruin of the French in Bengal. The chief French

Factories were, as I have said, at Chandernagore, Cossimbazar, and Dacca. The Chiefs of these Factories were M. Renault, the Director of all the French in Bengal; M. Law, a nephew of the celebrated Law of Lauriston, the financier; and M. Courtin. It is the doings and sufferings of these three gallant men which are recorded in the following chapters. They had no hope of being able to resist the English by themselves, but they hoped, and actually believed, that France would send them assistance if they could only hold out till it arrived. Renault, whose case was the most desperate, perhaps thought that the Nawab would, in his own interest, support him if the English attacked Chandernagore; but knowing the Nawab as well as he did, and reflecting that he had himself refused the Nawab assistance when he asked for it, his hope must have been a feeble one. Still he could not, with honour, give up a fortified position without attempting a defence, and he determined to do his best. When he failed, all that Law and Courtin could expect to do was to maintain their personal liberty and create a diversion in the north of Bengal when French forces attacked it in the south. It was not their fault that the attack was never made.

I shall make no mention of the fate of the Factories at Balasore and Jugdea. At these the number of Frenchmen was so very small that resistance and escape were equally hopeless. Patna lay on the line of Law's retreat, and, as we shall see, he was joined by the second and other subordinate officers of that Factory. The chief, M. de la Bretesche, was too ill to be moved, but he managed, by the assistance of his native friends, to secure a large portion of the property of the French East India Company, and so to finance Law during his wanderings.

NOTES:

[1: Aliverdi Khan entered Muxadavad or Murshidabad as a conqueror on the 30th of March, 1742. He died on the 10th of April, 1756. (*Scrafton*.)]

[2: Literally the fourth part of the Revenues. The Marathas extorted the right to levy this from the Emperor Aurengzebe, and under pretext of collecting it they ravaged a large portion of India.]

[3: Court, or Court officials and nobles.]

[4: Such fires are mentioned in many Indian legends. In the "Arabian Nights" we read of a demon changing himself into a flaming fire.]

[5: His age is stated by some as nineteen, by others as about twenty-five. See note, p. 66.]

[6: Amina Begum.]

[7: *Diwan*, i.e. Minister or Manager.]

[8: The English at Dacca surrendered to the Nawab of that place, and were afterwards released. Those at Jugdea and Balasore escaped direct to Fulta.]

[9: Captain George Minchin.]

[10: Known in history as the Black Hole of Calcutta.]

[11: Both stories may be true. Manik Chand was nearly

killed at the battle of Budge Budge by a bullet passing through his turban, and the incident of the ***nautch*** may have happened at Calcutta, where he certainly showed less courage.]

CHAPTER II
M. RENAULT, CHIEF OF CHANDERNAGORE

The French East India Company was founded in 1664, during the ministry of M. Colbert. Chandernagore, on the Ganges, or rather that mouth of it now known as the River Hugli, was founded in 1676; and in 1688 the town and territory were ceded to France by the Emperor Aurengzebe. I know of no plan of Chandernagore in the 17th century, and those of the 18th are extremely rare. Two or three are to be found in Paris, but the destruction of the Fort and many of the buildings by the English after its capture in 1757, and the decay of the town after its restoration to the French, owing to diminished trade, make it extremely difficult to recognize old landmarks. The Settlement, however, consisted of a strip of land, about two leagues in length and one in depth, on the right or western bank of the Hugli. Fort d'Orleans lay in the middle of the river front. It was commenced in 1691, and finished in 1693.[12] Facing the north was the Porte Royale, and to the east, or river-side, was the Water Gate. The north-eastern bastion was known as that of the Standard, or Pavillon. The north-western bastion was overlooked by the Jesuit Church, and the south-eastern by the Dutch Octagon. This last building was situated on one of a number of pieces of land which, though within the French bounds, belonged to the Dutch before the grant of the imperial charter, and which the Dutch had always refused to sell. The Factory buildings were in the Fort itself. To the west lay the Company's Tank, the hospitals, and the cemetery.

European houses, interspersed with native dwellings, lay all around.
M. d'Albert says that these houses were large and convenient, but
chiefly of one story only, built along avenues of fine trees, or
along the handsome quay. D'Albert also mentions a chapel in the
Fort,[13] the churches of the Jesuits and the Capucins, and some
miserable *pagodas* belonging to the Hindus, who, owing to the
necessity of employing them as clerks and servants, were allowed the
exercise of their religion. In his time the Europeans numbered about
500. There were besides some 400 Armenians, Moors[14] and Topasses,
1400 to 1500 Christians, including slaves, and 18,000 to 20,000
Gentiles, divided, he says, into 52 different castes or occupations.
It is to be supposed that the European houses had improved in the
thirty years since d'Albert's visit; at any rate many of those which
were close to the Fort now commanded its interior from their roofs
or upper stories, exactly as the houses of the leading officials in
Calcutta commanded the interior of Fort William. No other fact could
be so significant of the security which the Europeans in Bengal
believed they enjoyed from any attack by the forces of the native
Government. The site of the Fort is now covered with native huts.
The Cemetery still remains and the Company's Tank (now known as Lal
Dighi), whilst Kooti Ghat is the old landing-place of Fort
d'Orleans.

As regards the European population at the time of the siege we have
no definite information. The Returns drawn up by the French
officials at the time of the capitulation do not include the women
and children or the native and mixed population. The ladies,[15] and
it is to be presumed the other women also, for there is no mention
of women during the siege, retired to the Dutch and Danish
settlements at Chinsurah and Serampore a few days before, and the
native population disappeared as soon as the British army
approached. The Returns therefore show only 538 Europeans and 66
Topasses. The Governor or Director, as already mentioned, was Pierre

Renault: his Council consisted of MM. Fournier, Caillot, Laporterie, Nicolas, and Picques. There were 36 Frenchmen of lesser rank in the Company's service, as well as 6 surgeons. The troops were commanded by M. de Tury and 10 officers. There were also 10 officers of the French East India Company's vessels, and 107 persons of sufficient importance for their *parole* to be demanded when the Fort fell. Apparently these Returns do not include those who were killed in the defence, nor have we any definite information as to the number of French sepoys, but Eyre Coote[16] says there were 500.

The story of the siege is to be gathered from many accounts. M. Renault and his Council submitted an official report; Renault wrote many letters to Dupleix and other patrons or friends; several of the Council and other private persons did the same.[17] M. Jean Law, whose personal experiences we shall deal with in the next chapter, was Chief of Cossimbazar, and watched the siege, as it were, from the outside. His straightforward narrative helps us now and then to correct a mis-statement made by the besieged in the bitterness of defeat. On the English side, besides the Bengal records, there are Clive's and Eyre Coote's military journals, the Logs of the British ships of war, and the journal of Surgeon Edward Ives of His Majesty's ship *Kent*. Thus this passage of arms, almost the only one in Bengal[18] in which the protagonists were Europeans, is no obscure event, but one in which almost every incident was seen and described from opposite points of view. This multiplicity of authorities makes it difficult to form a connected narrative, and, in respect to many incidents, I shall have to follow that account which seems to enter into the fullest or most interesting detail.

It will now be necessary to go back a little. After the capture of Calcutta in June, 1756, the behaviour of the Nawab to all Europeans was so overbearing that Renault found it necessary to ask the Superior Council of Pondicherry for reinforcements, but all that he received was 67 Europeans and 167 Sepoys. No money was sent him, and every day he expected to hear that war had broken out between France and England.

"Full of these inquietudes, gentlemen, I was in the most cruel embarrassment, knowing not even what to desire. A strong detestation of the tyranny of the Nawab, and of the excesses which he was committing against Europeans, made me long for the arrival of the English in the Ganges to take vengeance for them. At the same time I feared the consequences of war being declared. In every letter M. de Leyrit[19] impressed upon me the necessity of fortifying Chandernagore as best I could, and of putting the town in a state of security against a surprise, but you have only to look at Chandernagore to see how difficult it was for us, absolutely destitute as we were of men and money, to do this with a town open on all sides, and with nothing even to mark it off from the surrounding country."[20]

He goes on to describe Fort d'Orleans--

"almost in the middle of the settlement, surrounded by houses, which command it, a square of about 600 feet,[21] built of brick, flanked with four bastions, with six guns each, without ramparts or glacis. The southern curtain, about 4 feet thick, not raised to its full height, was provided only with a battery of 3 guns; there was a similar battery to the west, but the rest of the west curtain was only a wall of mud and brick, about a foot and a half thick, and 8 or 10 feet high; there were warehouses ranged against the east curtain which faced the Ganges, and which was still in process of construction; the whole of this side had no ditch, and that round the other sides was dry, only 4

feet in depth, and a mere ravine. The walls of the Fort up
to the ramparts were 15 feet high, and the houses, on the
edge of the counterscarp, which commanded it, were as much
as 30 feet."

Perhaps the Fort was best defended on the west, where the Company's
Tank[22] was situated. Its bank was only about twelve feet from the
Fort Ditch. This use of tanks for defensive purposes was an
excellent one, as they also provided the garrison with a good supply
of drinking water. A little later Clive protected his great barracks
at Berhampur with a line of large tanks along the landward side.
However, this tank protected one side only, and the task of holding
such a fort with an inadequate garrison was not a hopeful one even
for a Frenchman. It was only his weakness which had made Renault
submit to pay the contribution demanded by the Nawab on his
triumphant return from Calcutta in July of the previous year, and he
and his comrades felt very bitterly the neglect of the Company in
not sending money and reinforcements. One of his younger
subordinates wrote to a friend in Pondicherry:[23]--

"But the 3-1/2 lahks that the Company has to pay to the
Nawab, is that a trifle? Yes, my dear fellow, for I should
like it to have to pay still more, to teach it how to leave
this Factory, which is, beyond contradiction, the finest of its
settlements, denuded of soldiers and munitions of war, so
that it is not possible for us to show our teeth."

The wish was prophetic.

Like the English the French were forbidden by the Nawab to fortify
themselves. Renault dared not pay attention to this order. He had
seen what had happened to the English by the neglect of proper
precautions, and when things were at their worst, the Nawab had to

seek his alliance against the English, grant him leave to fortify Chandernagore, and, later on, even to provide him with money under the pretence that he was simply restoring the sum forcibly extorted from him the previous year.[24] Trade was at a standstill, and Renault was determined that if the enemies of his nation were destined to take the Company's property, they should have the utmost difficulty possible in doing so. He expended the money on provisions and ammunition. At the same time, that he might not lose any chance of settling affairs peaceably with the English, he refused to associate himself with the Nawab, and entered upon negotiations for a neutrality in the Ganges. To protect himself if these failed, he began raising fortifications and pulling down the houses which commanded the Fort or masked its fire.

He could not pull down the houses on the south of the Fort, from which Clive subsequently made his attack, partly for want of time, partly because the native workmen ran away, and partly because of the bad feeling prevalent in the motley force which formed his garrison.[25] The most fatal defect of all was the want of a military engineer. The person who held that position had been sent from France. He was a master mason, and had no knowledge of engineering. It had been the same story in Calcutta. Drake's two engineers had been a subaltern in the military and a young covenanted servant. Renault had to supervise the fortifications himself.

"I commenced to pull down the church and the house of the Jesuit fathers, situated on the edge of the Ditch, also all the houses of private persons which masked the entire north curtain. The wood taken from the ruins of these served to construct a barrier extending from bastion to bastion and supporting this same north curtain, which seemed ready to fall to pieces from old age."

This barrier was placed four feet outside the wall, the intervening space being filled in with earth.

> "Also in front of Porte Royale" (i.e. outside the gate in the avenue), "the weakest side of the Fort, I placed a battery of 3 guns, and worked hard at clearing out and enlarging the Ditch, but there was no time to make it of any use as a defence. A warehouse on which I put bales of ***gunny***[26] to prevent cannon balls from breaking in the vaults of the roof, served it as a casemate."

The east or river curtain was left alone. The French were, in fact, so confident that the ships of war would not be able to force their way up the river, and that Clive would not therefore think of attacking on that side, that the only precaution they took at first was the erection of two batteries outside the Fort. It is a well-known maxim in war that one should attack at that point at which the enemy deems himself most secure, and it will be seen that all Clive's efforts were aimed at preparing for Admiral Watson to attack on the east.

As regards artillery Renault was better off.

> "The alarm which the Prince" (Siraj-ud-daula) "gave us in June last having given me reason to examine into the state of the artillery, I found that not one of the carriages of the guns on the ramparts was in a serviceable condition, not a field-piece mounted, not a platform ready for the mortars. I gave all my attention to these matters, and fortunately had time to put them right."

To serve his guns Renault had the sailors of the Company's ship, ***Saint Contest***, whose commander, M. de la Vigne Buisson, was the soul of the defence.

About this time he received a somewhat doubtful increase to his
garrison, a crowd of deserters from the English East India Company's
forces. The latter at this time were composed of men of all
nationalities, English, Germans, Swiss, Dutch, and even French. Many
of them, and naturally the foreigners especially, were ready to
desert upon little provocation. The hardships of service in a
country where the climate and roads were execrable, where food and
pay were equally uncertain, and where promises were made not to be
kept, were provocations which the best soldiers might have found it
difficult to resist. We read of whole regiments in the English and
French services refusing to obey orders, and of mutinies of officers
as well as of men. The one reward of service was the chance of
plunder, and naturally, then, as soon as the fighting with the Nawab
had stopped for a time, the desertions from the British forces were
numerous. Colonel Clive had more than once written to Renault to
remonstrate with him for taking British soldiers into his service.
Probably Renault could have retorted the accusation with justice--at
any rate, he went on enlisting deserters; and from those who had now
come over he formed a company of grenadiers of 50 men, one of
artillery of 30, and one of sailors of 60, wisely giving them a
little higher pay than usual, "to excite their emulation." One of
these was a man named Lee,--

"a corporal and a deserter from the *Tyger*, who pledged
himself to the enemy that he would throw two shells out of
three into the *Tyger*, but whilst he was bringing the mortars
to bear for that purpose, he was disabled by a musket bullet
from the *Kent's* tops. He was afterwards sent home a
prisoner to England."[27]

As might be expected the younger Frenchmen were wild with delight at the chance of seeing a good fight. Some of them had been much disappointed that the Nawab had not attacked Chandernagore in June, 1756. One of them wrote[28]--

"I was charmed with the adventure and the chance
of carrying a musket, having always had" (what Frenchman
hasn't?) "a secret leaning towards a military life. I
intended to kill a dozen Moors myself in the first sortie we
made, for I was determined not to stand like a stock on a
bastion, where one only runs the risk of getting wounds
without having any of the pleasure of inflicting them."

If not the highest form of military spirit, this was at any rate one of which a good commander might make much use. Renault took advantage of this feeling, and from the young men of the colony, such as Company's servants, ships' officers, supercargoes, and European inhabitants,[29] he made a company of volunteers, to whom, at their own request, he gave his son, an officer of the garrison, as commander.

One of the volunteer officers writes:--

"I had the honour to be appointed lieutenant, and was
much pleased when I saw the spirit of emulation which
reigned in every heart. I cannot sufficiently praise the
spirit of exactitude with which every one was animated, and
the progress which all made in so short a time in the
management of their arms. I lay stress on the fact that it
was an occupation entirely novel to them, and one of which
the commencement always appears very hard, but they overcame
all difficulties, and found amusement in what to others
would appear merely laborious."

All this time Renault was watching the war between the English and the Moors. In January the English sailed up the Hugli, passed Chandernagore contemptuously without a salute, burned the Moorish towns of Hugli and Bandel, ravaged the banks of the river, and retired to Calcutta. Up to this the Nawab had not condescended to notice the English; now, in a moment of timidity, he asked the intervention of the French as mediators.[30] Renault eagerly complied, for had his mediation been accepted, he would have inserted in the treaty a clause enforcing peace amongst the Europeans in Bengal; but the English refused to treat through the French. This could have only one meaning. Renault felt that his course was now clear, and was on the point of offering the alliance which the Nawab had so long sought for, when he received orders from M. de Leyrit forbidding him to attack the English by land. As M. Law writes, if Renault had been free to join the Nawab with 500 Europeans, either Clive would not have ventured a night attack on the Nawab's camp, or, had he done so, the event would probably have been very different. Under the circumstances, all that Renault could do was to continue his fortifications. It was now that he first realized that Admiral Watson would take part in the attack.

"As the ships of war were what we had most to fear from, we constructed on the river bank a battery of 6 guns, four of which covered the approach to the Fort. From the foot of the battery a bank twenty-two feet high stretching to the Fort, was begun, so as to protect the curtain on this side from the fire of the ships, *but it was not finished*. We had also to attend to the inhabited portion of the town; it was impossible to do more, but we determined to protect it from a surprise, and so ditches were dug across the streets and outposts established."[31]

It was this waste of valuable time upon the defence of the town that

a capable engineer would have saved Renault from the mistake of
committing. Had he limited his efforts to strengthening the walls of
the Fort and cleared away the surrounding houses, he would have been
not only stronger against the attack of the land force, but also in
a much better position to resist the ships.

The issue of the Nawab's attack on Calcutta has already been told.
He was so depressed by his failure that he now treated Renault with
the greatest respect, and it was now that he gave him the sum of
money--a lakh of rupees, then worth L12,500--which he spent on
provisions and munitions of war. Renault says:--

"The Nawab's envoy further gave me to understand that
he was, in his heart, enraged with the English, and continued
to regard them as his enemies. In spite of this we saw
clearly from the treaty just made" (with the English)
"that we should be its victims, and knowing Siraj-ud-daula's
character, his promise to assist me strongly if the
English attacked us did not quiet my mind. I prepared for
whatever might happen by pressing on our preparations and
collecting all kinds of provisions in the Fort."

The Nawab and the English concluded a treaty of peace and alliance
on the 9th of February, 1757. Renault mentions no actual treaty
between the Nawab and the French, but the French doctor referred to
in a note above asserts that the Nawab demanded that the Council
should bind itself in writing.

"to oppose the passage of the English past Chandernagore....
It was merely engaging to defend ourselves against
the maritime force of the English ... because Chandernagore
was the only place on this coast against which they
could undertake any enterprise by water. This engagement

was signed and sent to the Nawab three days after he had made peace with the English. The Council received in reply two privileges, the one to coin money with the King's stamp at Chandernagore, the other liberty of trade for individual Frenchmen on the same footing as the Company, and 100,000 rupees on account of the 300,000 which he had extorted the previous year."

It does not matter whether this engagement was signed or not.[32] As a Frenchman thus mentions it, the rumour of its signature must have been very strong. It is probable that the English heard of it, and believed it to be conclusive proof of the secret understanding between the Nawab and the French. The privilege of individual trade was particularly likely to excite their commercial jealousy, for it was to this very privilege in their own case that the wealth and strength of Calcutta were due. Such a rumour, therefore, was not likely to facilitate negotiations. Nevertheless, Renault sent MM. Fournier and Nicolas, the latter of whom had many friends amongst the English, to Calcutta, to re-open the negotiations for a neutrality. These negotiations seemed to be endless. The most striking feature was Admiral Watson's apparent vacillation. When the Council proposed war he wanted peace, when they urged neutrality he wanted war. Clive went so far as to present a memorial to the Council, saying it was unfair to continue the negotiations if the Admiral was determined not to agree to a treaty. It seems as if the Council wanted war, but wished to throw the responsibility upon the Admiral. On the other hand the Admiral was only too eager to fight, but hesitated to involve the Company in a war with the French and the Nawab combined, at a moment when the British land forces were so weakened by disease that success might be considered doubtful. He had also to remember the fact that the Council at Chandernagore was subordinate to the Council at Pondicherry, and the latter might, whenever convenient to the French, repudiate the treaty. However, in spite of all difficulties, the terms were agreed to, the draft was prepared, and only the signatures were wanting, when a large reinforcement of Europeans arrived from Bombay, and the Admiral received formal notification of the declaration of war, and orders from the Admiralty to attack the French.[33] This put an immediate end to negotiations, and the envoys were instructed to return to Chandernagore. At the same time the English determined to try and prevent the Nawab from joining the French.

Whilst the Admiral was making up his mind fortune had favoured the English. The Nawab, in fear of an invasion of Bengal by the Pathans, had called upon the British for assistance, and on the 3rd of March Clive's army left Calcutta **en route** for Murshidabad. The Admiral now pointed out to the Nawab that the British could not safely leave Chandernagore behind them in the hands of an enemy, and Clive wrote to the same effect, saying he would wait near Chandernagore for a reply. On the 10th of March the Nawab wrote a letter to the Admiral, which concluded with the following significant words:--

"You have understanding and generosity: if your enemy with an upright heart claims your protection, you will give him life, but then you must be **well** satisfied of the innocence of his intentions: if not, whatever you think right, that do."

Law says this letter was a forgery,[34] but as the Nawab did not write any letters himself, the only test of authenticity was his seal, which was duly attached. The English believed it to be genuine, and the words quoted could have but one meaning. Admiral Watson read them as a permission to attack the French without fear of the Nawab's interference. He prepared to support Clive as soon as the water in the Hugli would allow his ships to pass up, and, it must be supposed, informed Clive of the letter he had received. At any rate, he so informed the Council.

Clive reached Chandernagore on the 12th, and probably heard on that day or the next from Calcutta. On the 13th he sent the following summons--which Renault does not mention, and did not reply to--to Chandernagore:--

"SIR,

"The King of Great Britain having declared war against France, I summons you in his name to surrender the Fort of Chandernagore. In case of refusal you are to answer the consequences, and expect to be treated according to the usage of war in such cases.

"I have the honour to be, sir,

"Your most obedient and humble servant,

"ROBERT CLIVE."

It is important, in the light of what happened later, to notice that Clive addresses Renault as a combatant and the head of the garrison.

In England we have recently seen men eager to vilify their own nation. France has produced similar monsters. One of them wrote from Pondicherry:--

"The English having changed their minds on the arrival of the reinforcement from Bombay, our gentlemen at Chandernagore prepared to ransom themselves, and they would have done so at whatever price the ransom had been fixed provided anything had remained to them. That mode of agreement could not possibly suit the taste of the English.

It was rejected, and the Council of Chandernagore had no other resource except to surrender on the best conditions they could obtain from the generosity of their enemy. This course was so firmly resolved upon that they gave no thought to defending themselves. The military insisted only on firing a single discharge, which they desired the Council would grant them. It was only the marine and the citizens who, though they had no vote in the Council, cried out tumultuously that the Fort must be defended. A plot was formed to prevent the Director's son, who was ready to carry the keys of the town to the English camp, from going out. Suddenly some one fired a musket. The English thought it was the reply to their summons. They commenced on their side to fire their artillery, and that was how a defence which lasted ten whole days was begun."

How much truth is contained in the above paragraph may be judged by what has been already stated. It will be sufficient to add that Clive, receiving no answer to his summons, made a sudden attack on a small earthwork to the south-west of the fort at 3 A.M. on the 14th of March. For two whole days then, the English had been in sight of Chandernagore without attacking. The French ladies had been sent to Chinsurah and Serampore, so that the defenders had nothing to fear on their account. Besides the French soldiers and civilians, there were also about 2000 Moorish troops present, whom Law says he persuaded the Nawab to send down as soon as the English left Calcutta. Other accounts say that Renault hired them to assist him. The Nawab had a strong force at Murshidabad ready to march under one of his commanders, Rai Durlabh Ram; but the latter had experienced what even a small English force could do in the night attack on the Nawab's camp, and was by no means inclined to match himself a second time against Clive; accordingly, he never got further than five leagues from Murshidabad. Urgent messages were sent from

Chandernagore as soon as the attack began. M. Law begged of the Nawab to send reinforcements. Mr. Watts, the English Chief, and all his party in the **Durbar**, did their utmost to prevent any orders being issued. The Nawab gave orders which he almost immediately countermanded. Renault ascribes this to a letter which he says Clive wrote on the 14th of March, the very day of the attack, promising the Nawab to leave the French alone, but it is not at all likely that he did so. It is true Clive had written to this effect on the 22nd of February; but since then much had happened, and he was now acting, as he thought and said, with the Nawab's permission. On the 16th of March he wrote to Nand Kumar, Faujdar[35] of Hugli, as follows:--

"The many deceitful wicked measures that the French have taken to endeavour to deprive me of the Nawab's favour (tho' I thank God they have proved in vain, since his Excellency's friendship towards me is daily increasing) has long made me look on them as enemies to the English, but I could no longer stifle my resentment when I found that ... they dared to oppose the freedom of the English trade on the Ganges by seizing a boat with an English *dustuck*,[36] and under English colours that was passing by their town. I am therefore come to a resolution to attack them. I am told that some of the Government's forces have been perswaded under promise of great rewards from the French to join them against us; I should be sorry, at a time when I am so happy in his Excellency's favour and friendship, that I should do any injury to his servants; I am therefore to desire you will send these forces an order to withdraw, and that no other may come to their assistance."[37]

What Clive feared was that, though the Nawab might not interfere openly, some of his

servants might receive secret orders to do so, and
on the 22nd of March he wrote even more curtly
to Rai Durlabh himself:--

"I hear you are arrived within 20 miles of Hughly.
Whether you come as a friend or an enemy, I know not. If
as the latter, say so at once, and I will send some people out
to fight you immediately.... Now you know my mind."[38]

When diplomatic correspondence was conducted in letters of this
kind, it is easy to understand that the Nawab was frightened out of
his wits, and absolutely unable to decide what course he should
take. There was little likelihood of the siege being influenced by
anything he might do.

The outpost mentioned as the object of the first attack was a small
earthwork, erected at the meeting of three roads. It was covered by
the Moorish troops, who held the roofs of the houses around. As the
intention of the outposts was merely to prevent the town from being
surprised, and to enable the inhabitants to take shelter in the
Fort, the outpost ought to have been withdrawn as quickly as
possible, but, probably because they thought it a point of honour
to make a stout defence wherever they were first attacked,
the defenders stood to it gallantly. Renault sent repeated
reinforcements, first the company of grenadiers, then at 9 o'clock
the company of artillery, and at 10 o'clock, when the surrounding
houses were in flames, and many of the Moors had fled, a company of
volunteers. With these, and a further reinforcement of sixty
sailors, the little fort held out till 7 o'clock in the evening,
when the English, after three fruitless assaults, ceased fire and
withdrew. Street fighting is always confusing, and hence the
following vague description of the day's events from Captain Eyre
Coote's journal:--

"Colonel Clive ordered the picquets, with the company's
grenadiers, to march into the French bounds, which is encompassed
with an old ditch,[39] the entrance into it a gateway
with embrasures on the top but no cannons, which the
French evacuated on our people's advancing. As soon as
Captain Lynn, who commanded the party, had taken possession,
he acquainted the Colonel, who ordered Major Kilpatrick
and me, with my company of grenadiers, to join Captain
Lynn, and send him word after we had reconnoitred the
place. On our arrival there we found a party of French was
in possession of a road leading to a redoubt that they had
thrown up close under their fort, where they had a battery
of cannon, and upon our advancing down the road, they fired
some shots at us. We detached some parties through a wood,
and drove them from the road into their batteries with the
loss of some men; we then sent for the Colonel, who, as soon
as he joined us, sent to the camp for more troops. We
continued firing at each other in an irregular manner till
about noon, at which time the Colonel ordered me to continue
with my grenadier company and about 200 sepoys at the
advance post, and that he would go with the rest of our
troops to the entrance, which was about a mile back. About
2 o'clock word was brought me that the French were making
a sortie. Soon after, I perceived the sepoys retiring from
their post, upon which I sent to the Colonel to let him know
the French were coming out. I was then obliged to divide
my company, which consisted of about 50 men, into 2 or 3
parties (very much against my inclination) to take possession
of the ground the sepoys had quitted. We fired pretty
warmly for a quarter of an hour from the different parties
at each other, when the French retreated again into their
battery. On this occasion I had a gentleman (Mr. Tooke[40]),
who was a volunteer, killed, and 2 of my men wounded.

The enemy lost 5 or 6 Europeans and some blacks. I got
close under the battery, and was tolerably well sheltered by
an old house, where I continued firing till about 7 o'clock,
at which time I was relieved, and marched back to camp."

The defenders were much exhausted, as well by the fighting as by the
smoke and heat from the burning houses and the heat of the weather,
for it was almost the hottest season of the year. It seemed probable
that the English would make another attack during the night, and as
the defenders already amounted to a very large portion of the
garrison, it was almost impossible to reinforce them without
leaving the Fort itself in great danger, if Clive managed to
approach it from any other quarter. Renault called a council of war,
and, after taking the opinion of his officers in writing to the
effect that the outposts must be abandoned, he withdrew the
defenders at 9 o'clock, under cover of the darkness: The French had
suffered a loss of only 10 men killed and wounded. Clive mentions
that, at the same time, all the other outposts and batteries, except
those on the river side, were withdrawn.

Mustering his forces in the Fort, Renault found them to be composed
of 237 soldiers (of whom 117 were deserters from the British), 120
sailors, 70 half-castes and private Europeans, 100 persons employed
by the Company, 167 Sepoys and 100 *Topasses*. Another French
account puts the total of the French garrison at 489, but this
probably excludes many of the private people.[41]

On the 15th the English established themselves in the town, and
drove out the Moors who had been stationed on the roofs of the
houses. This gave them to some extent the command of the interior of
the Fort, but no immediate attack was made on the latter. A French
account[42] says this was because--

"all their soldiers were drunk with the wine they had found
in the houses. Unfortunately we did not know of this. It
would have been the moment to make a sortie, of which the
results must have been favourable to us, the enemy being
incapable of defence."

During the night of the 15th the Fort was bombarded, and on the
morning of the 16th the British completed the occupation of the
houses deserted by the Moors. The latter not being received into the
Fort, either fled or were sent away. They betook themselves to Nand
Kumar, the Faujdar of Hugli, announcing the capture of the town.
Nand Kumar, who is said to have had an understanding with the
British, sent on the message to Rai Durlabh and the Nawab, with the
malicious addition that the Fort, if it had not already fallen,
would fall before Rai Durlabh could reach it. This put an end to all
chance of the Nawab interfering.

The French spent the day in blocking a narrow passage formed by a
sandbank in the river, a short distance below the town. They sank--

"four large ships and a hulk,... and had a chain and boom
across in order to prevent our going up with the squadron.
Captain Toby sent his 2nd lieutenant, Mr. Bloomer, that night,
who cut the chain and brought off a sloop that buoyed it up."[43]

It was apparently this rapid attack on the position that accounts
for the timidity of the pilots and boatmen, who, Renault tells us,
hurried away without staying to sink two other ships which were half
laden, and which, if sunk, would have completely blocked the
passage. Even on the ships which were sunk the masts had been left
standing, so as to point out their position to the enemy.

Besides the ships sunk in the passage, there were at Chandernagore the French East Indiaman the **Saint Contest** (Captain de la Vigne Buisson), four large ships, and several small ones. The French needed all the sailors for the Fort, so they sank all the vessels they could not send up the river except three, which it was supposed they intended to use as fire-ships.

Clive, in the meantime, was advancing cautiously, his men erecting batteries, which seemed to be very easily silenced by the superior gunnery of the Fort. His object was partly to weary out the garrison by constant fighting, and partly to creep round to the river face, so as to be in a position to take the batteries which commanded the narrow river passage, as soon as Admiral Watson was ready to attack the Fort. Later on, the naval officers asserted he could not have taken the Fort without the assistance of the fleet. He said he could, and it is certain that if he had had no fleet to assist him his mode of attack would have been a very different one.

Early in the siege the French were warned from Chinsurah to beware of treachery amongst the deserters in their pay, and on the 17th of March a number of arrows were found in the Fort with labels attached, bearing the words:--

"Pardon to deserters who will rejoin their colours, and rewards to officers who will come over to us."

These were seized by the officers before the men could see them, but one of the officers themselves, Charles Cossard de Terraneau, a sub-lieutenant of the garrison, took advantage of the offer to go over to the English. This officer had served with credit in the South of India, and had lost an arm in his country's service. The reason of his desertion is said to have been a quarrel with M. Renault. M. Raymond, the translator of a native history of the time by Gholam Husain Khan,[44] tells a story of De Terraneau which seems improbable. It is to the effect that he betrayed the secret of the river passage to Admiral Watson, and that a few years later he sent home part of the reward of his treachery to his father in France. The old man returned the money with indignant comments on his son's conduct, and De Terraneau committed suicide in despair. As a matter of fact, De Terraneau was a land officer,[45] and therefore not likely to be able to advise the Admiral, who, as we shall see, solved the riddle of the passage in a perfectly natural manner, and the Probate Records show that De Terraneau lived till 1765, and in his will left his property to his wife Ann, so the probability is that he lived and died quietly in the British service. His only trouble seems to have been to get himself received by his new brother officers. However, he was, so Clive tells us, the only artillery officer the French had, and his desertion was a very serious matter. Renault writes:--

"The same night, by the improved direction of the besiegers' bombs, I had no doubt but that he had done us a bad service."

On the 18th the French destroyed a battery which the English had established near the river, and drove them out of a house opposite the south-east bastion. The same day the big ships of the squadron--the **Kent** (Captain Speke), the **Tyger** (Captain Latham), and the **Salisbury** (Captain Martin), appeared below the town. The **Bridgewater** and **Kingfisher** had come up before. Admiral Watson was on board the **Kent**, and Admiral Pocock on the **Tyger**. The fleet anchored out of range of the Fort at the Prussian Gardens, a mile and a half below the town, and half a mile below the narrow passage in which the ships had been sunk.

On the 19th Admiral Watson formally announced the declaration of war,[46] and summoned the Fort to surrender. The Governor called a council of war, in which there was much difference of opinion. Some thought the Admiral would not have come so far without his being certain of his ability to force the passage; indeed the presence of so many deserters in the garrison rendered it probable that he had secret sources of information. As a matter of fact, it was only when Lieutenant Hey, the officer who had brought the summons, and, in doing so, had rowed between the masts of the sunken vessels, returned to the *Kent*, that Admiral Watson knew the passage was clear. Renault and the Council were aware that the Fort could not resist the big guns of the ships, and accordingly the more thoughtful members of the council of war determined, if possible, to try and avoid fighting by offering a ransom. This apparently gave rise to the idea that they wished to surrender, and an English officer says:--

"Upon the Admiral's sending them a summons ... to surrender, they were very stout; they gave us to understand there were two parties in the Factory, the Renaultions and the anti-Renaultions. The former, which they called the great-wigg'd gentry, or councillors, were for giving up the Fort, but the others vowed they would die in the breach. To these high and lofty expressions the Admiral could give no other answer than that in a very few days, or hours perhaps, he would give them a very good opportunity of testifying their zeal for the Company and the Grand Monarque."

The offer of ransom was made, and was refused by the Admiral. Renault says, he--

"insisted on our surrendering and the troops taking possession of the Fort, promising, however, that every one should keep his own property. There was not a man amongst us who did not prefer to run the risk of whatever might happen to surrendering in this fashion, without the Fort having yet suffered any material damage, and every one was willing to risk his own interests in order to defend those of the Company. Every one swore to do his best."

The Admiral could not attack at once, owing to the state of the river, but to secure his own position against any counter-attack, such as was very likely with a man like Captain de la Vigne in the Fort, he sent up boats the same night, and sank the vessels which it was supposed the French intended to use as fire-ships; and the next day Mr. John Delamotte, master of the **Kent**, under a heavy fire, sounded and buoyed the passage for the ships.

The army, meanwhile, continued its monotonous work ashore, the soldiers building batteries for the French to knock to pieces, but succeeding in Clive's object, which was "to keep the enemy constantly awake."[47] Sometimes this work was dangerous, as, for instance, on the 21st, when a ball from the Fort knocked down a verandah close to one of the English batteries, "the rubbish of which choked up one of our guns, very much bruised two artillery officers, and buried several men in the ruins."[48]

By the 22nd Clive had worked his way round to the river, and was established to the north-east and south-east of the Fort so as to assist the Admiral, and on the river the Admiral had at last got the high tide he was waiting for. Surgeon Ives tells the story as follows:[49]--

"The Admiral the same evening ordered lights to be placed on the masts of the vessels that had been sunk, with blinds towards the Fort, that we might see how to pass between them a little before daylight, and without being discovered by the enemy.

"At length the glorious morning of the 23rd of March arrived." Clive's men gallantly stormed the battery covering the narrow pass,[50] "and upon the ships getting under sail the Colonel's battery, which had been finished behind a dead wall," to take off the fire of the Fort when the ships passed up, began firing away, and had almost battered down the corner of the south-east bastion before the ships arrived within shot of the Fort. "The *Tyger*, with Admiral Pocock's flag flying, took the lead, and about 6 o'clock in the morning got very well into her station against the north-east bastion. The *Kent*, with Admiral Watson's flag flying, quickly followed her, but before she could reach her proper station, the tide of ebb unfortunately made down the river, which occasioned her anchor to drag, so that before she brought up she had fallen abreast of the south-east bastion, the place where the *Salisbury* should have been, and from her mainmast aft she was exposed to the flank guns of the south-west bastion also. The accident of the *Kent's* anchor not holding fast, and her driving down into the *Salisbury's* station, threw this last ship out of action, to the great mortification of the captain, officers, and crew, for she never had it in her power to fire a gun, unless it was now and then, when she could sheer on the tide. The French, during the whole time of the *Kent* and *Tyger's* approach towards the Fort, kept up a terrible cannonade upon them, without any resistance on their part; but as soon as the ships came properly to an anchor they returned it with such fury as astonished their adversaries. Colonel Clive's troops at the same time got into those houses which were nearest the Fort, and from thence greatly annoyed the enemy with their musketry. Our ships lay so near to the Fort that the musket balls fired from their tops, by striking against the

chunam[51] walls of the Governor's palace, which was in
the very centre of the Fort, were beaten as flat as a half-crown.
The fire now became general on both sides, and was
kept up with extraordinary spirit. The flank guns of the
south-west bastion galled the *Kent* very much, and the
Admiral's aide-de-camps being all wounded, Mr. Watson went
down himself to Lieutenant William Brereton, who commanded
the lower deck battery, and ordered him particularly
to direct his fire against those guns, and they were accordingly
soon afterwards silenced. At 8 in the morning
several of the enemy's shot struck the *Kent* at the same
time; one entered near the foremast, and set fire to two or
three 32-pound cartridges of gunpowder, as the boys held
them in their hands ready to charge the guns. By the explosion,
the wad-nets and other loose things took fire between
decks, and the whole ship was so filled with smoke that the
men, in their confusion, cried out she was on fire in the
gunner's store-room, imagining from the shock they had
felt from the balls that a shell had actually fallen into her.
This notion struck a panic into the greater part of the crew,
and 70 or 80 jumped out of the port-holes into the boats
that were alongside the ship. The French presently saw
this confusion on board the *Kent*, and, resolving to take the
advantage, kept up as hot a fire as possible upon her during
the whole time. Lieutenant Brereton, however, with the
assistance of some other brave men, soon extinguished the
fire, and then running to the ports, he begged the seamen to
come in again, upbraiding them for deserting their quarters;
but finding this had no effect upon them, he thought the
more certain method of succeeding would be to strike them
with a sense of shame, and therefore loudly exclaimed, 'Are
you Britons? You Englishmen, and fly from danger? For
shame! For shame!' This reproach had the desired effect;

to a man they immediately returned into the ship, repaired
to their quarters, and renewed a spirited fire on the enemy.

"In about three hours from the commencement of the
attack the parapets of the north and south bastions were
almost beaten down; the guns were mostly dismounted, and
we could plainly see from the main-top of the *Kent* that the
ruins from the parapet and merlons had entirely blocked up
those few guns which otherwise might have been fit for
service. We could easily discern, too, that there had been
a great slaughter among the enemy, who, finding that our
fire against them rather increased, hung out the white flag,
whereupon a cessation of hostilities took place, and the
Admiral sent Lieutenant Brereton (the only commissioned
officer on board the *Kent* that was not killed or wounded)
and Captain Coote of the King's regiment with a flag of truce
to the Fort, who soon returned, accompanied by the French
Governor's son, with articles of capitulation, which being
settled by the Admiral and Colonel, we soon after took possession
of the place."

So far then from the besiegers' side; Renault's description of the
fight is as follows:--

"The three largest vessels, aided by the high-water of
the equinoctial tides, which, moreover, had moved the vessels
sunk in the narrow passage, passed over the sunken ships,
which did not delay them for a moment, to within half
pistol shot of the Fort, and opened fire at 6 a.m. Then the
troops in the battery on the bank of the Ganges, who had
so far fired only one discharge, suddenly found themselves
overwhelmed with the fire from the tops of the ships,
abandoned it, and had much difficulty in gaining the Fort...

I immediately sent the company of grenadiers, with a detachment
of the artillery company as reinforcements, to the
south-eastern bastion and the Bastion du Pavillon, which two
bastions face the Ganges; but those troops under the fire of
the ships, joined to that of the land batteries, rebuilt the
same night, and of more than 3000 men placed on the roofs
of houses which overlooked the Fort, almost all took flight,
leaving two of their officers behind, one dead and the other
wounded. I was obliged to send immediately all the marine
and the inhabitants from the other posts.

"The attack was maintained with vigour from 6 a.m. to
10.30, when all the batteries were covered with dead and
wounded, the guns dismounted, and the merlons destroyed,
in spite of their being strengthened with bales of cloth. No
one could show himself on the bastions, demolished by the
fire of more than 100 guns; the troops were terrified during
this attack by the loss of all the gunners and of nearly
200 men; the bastions were undermined, and threatened to
crumble away and make a breach, which the exhaustion of
our people, and the smallness of the number who remained,
made it impossible for us to hope to defend successfully.
Not a soldier would put his hand to a gun; it was only the
European marine who stood to their duty, and half of these
were already killed or disabled. A body of English troops,
lying flat on the ground behind the screen which we had commenced
to erect on the bank of the Ganges, was waiting the
signal to attack. Seeing the impossibility of holding out longer,
I thought that in the state in which the Fort was I could not
in prudence expose it to an assault. Consequently I hoisted
the white flag and ordered the drums to beat a parley."

According to an account written later by a person who was not present at the siege, Renault lost his Fort by a quarter of an hour. This writer says the tide was rapidly falling, and, had the eastern defences of the Fort been able to resist a little longer, the ships would have found their lower tiers of guns useless, and might have been easily destroyed by the French. Suppositions of this kind always suppose a stupidity on the part of the enemy which Renault had no right to count upon. Admiral Watson must have known the strength of the fortress he was about to attack before he placed his ships in a position from which it would be impossible to withdraw them whenever he wished to do so.

The flag of truce being displayed, Captain Eyre Coote was sent ashore, and returned in a quarter of an hour with the Governor's son bearing "a letter concerning the delivery of the place." Articles were agreed upon, and about 3 o'clock in the afternoon Captain Coote, with a company of artillery and two companies of grenadiers, took possession of the Fort. Before this took place there occurred an event the consequences of which were very unfortunate for the French. Everything was in a state of confusion, and the deserters, who formed the majority of the garrison, expecting no mercy from the Admiral and Clive, determined to escape. Rushing tumultuously to the Porte Royale, their arms in their hands, they forced it to be opened to them, and, finding the northern road to Chinsurah unguarded, made the best of their way in that direction. They were accompanied by a number of the military and marine, as well as by some of the Company's servants and private persons who were determined not to surrender. As all this took place after the hoisting of the white flag and pending the conclusion of the capitulation, the English considered it a breach of the laws of warfare, and when later on the meaning of the capitulation itself was contested they absolutely refused to listen to any of the representations of the French. In all about 150 persons left the Fort. They had agreed to reassemble

at a place a little above Hugli. The English sent a small force
after them, who shot some and captured others, but about 80 officers
and men arrived at the rendezvous in safety. The pursuit, however,
was carried further, and Law writes:--

"Constantly pursued, they had to make forced marches.
Some lost their way; others, wearied out, were caught as they
stopped to rest themselves. However, when I least expected
it, I was delighted to see the officers and many of the soldiers
arrive in little bands of 5 and 6, all naked, and so worn out
that they could hardly hold themselves upright. Most of
them had lost their arms."

This reinforcement increased Law's garrison from 10 or 12 men to 60,
and secured the safety of his person, but the condition of the
fugitives must have been an object lesson to the Nawab and his
Durbar which it was not wise for the French to set before them. A
naval officer writes:--

"From the letters that have lately passed between the
Nawab and us, we have great reason to hope he will not
screen the French at all at Cossimbazar or Dacca. I only
wish the Colonel does not alarm him too much, by moving
with the army to the northward, I do assure you he is so
sufficiently frightened that he had rather encounter the new
Mogul[52] himself than accept our assistance, though he strenuously
begged for it about three weeks ago. He writes word
he needs no fuller assurance of our friendship for him, when
a single letter brought us so far on the road to Murshidabad
as Chandernagore."[53]

The escape of the French from Chandernagore is of interest, as it
shows the extraordinary condition of the country. It is probable

that the peasantry and gentry were indifferent as to whether the English or the French were victorious, whilst the local authorities were so paralyzed by the Nawab's hesitation that they did not know which side to assist. Later on we shall find that small parties, and even solitary Frenchmen, wandered through the country with little or no interference, though the English had been recognized as the friends and allies of the new Nawab, Mir Jafar.

To return, however, to Renault and the garrison of Chandernagore. The capitulation proposed by Renault and the Admiral's answers were to the following effect:--

1. The lives of the deserters to be spared. ***Answer***. The deserters to surrender absolutely.

2. Officers of the garrison to be prisoners on parole, and allowed to keep their effects. ***Answer***. Agreed to.

3. Soldiers of the garrison to be prisoners of war. ***Answer***. Agreed to, on condition that foreigners may enter the English service.

4. Sepoys of the garrison to be set free. ***Answer***. Agreed to.

5. Officers and crew of the French Company's ship to be sent to Pondicherry. ***Answer***. These persons to be prisoners of war according to articles 2 and 3.

6. The Jesuit fathers to be allowed to practise their religion and retain their property. ***Answer***. No European to be allowed to remain at Chandernagore, but the fathers to be allowed to retain their property.

7. All inhabitants to retain their property. ***Answer***. This to be

left to the Admiral's sense of equity.

8. The French Factories up-country to be left in the hands of their present chiefs. *Answer*. This to be settled by the Nawab and the Admiral.

9. The French Company's servants to go where they please, with their clothes and linen. *Answer*. Agreed to.

It is evident that the capitulation was badly drawn up. Civilians who had taken part in the defence, as had all the Company's servants, might be justly included in the garrison, and accordingly Admiral Watson and Clive declared they were all prisoners of war, and that article 9 merely permitted them to reside where they pleased on *parole*. On the other hand, Renault and the French Council declared that, being civilians, nothing could make them part of the garrison, and therefore under article 9 they might do what they pleased. Accordingly, they expressed much surprise when they were stopped at the Fort gates by one of Clive's officers, and forced to sign, before they were allowed to pass, a paper promising not to act against Britain directly or indirectly during the course of the war.

Another point of difficulty was in reference to article 7. The town had been in the hands of the British soldiers and sepoys for days. Much had been plundered, and both soldiers and sailors were wild for loot. They considered that the Admiral was acting unjustly to them in restoring their property to civilians who had been offered the chance of retaining it if they would avoid unnecessary bloodshed by a prompt surrender. Instead of this, the defence was so desperate that one officer writes:--

"Our losses have been very great, and we have never
yet obtained a victory at so dear a rate. Perhaps you will
hear of few instances where two ships have met with heavier
damage than the **Kent** and **Tyger** in this engagement."[54]

Clive's total loss was only about 40 men killed and wounded, but
the loss on the ships was so great, that before the Fort surrendered
the besiegers had lost quite as many men as the besieged, and it was
by no means clear to the common mind what claim the French had to
leniency. Even English officers wrote:--

"The Messieurs themselves deserve but little mercy from
us for their mean behaviour in setting fire to so many bales
of cloth and raw silk in the Fort but a very few minutes
before we entered, and it grieves us much, to see such a
number of stout and good vessels sunk with their whole
cargoes far above the Fort, which is a great loss to us and
no profit to them. Those indeed below, to hinder our passage
were necessary, the others were *merely through mischief*.
But notwithstanding this they scarcely ask a favour from
the Admiral but it is granted."

The result was that the soldiers on guard began to beat the coolies
who were helping the French to secure their goods, until they were
induced by gifts to leave them alone, and much plundering went on
when the soldiers could manage to escape notice. On one day three
black soldiers were executed, and on another Sergeant Nover[55] and
a private soldier of the 39th Regiment were condemned to death, for
breaking open the Treasury and stealing 3000 rupees. Another theft,
which was not traced, was the holy vessels and treasure of the
Church.

Many individual Frenchmen were ruined. Of one of these Surgeon Ives narrates the following pleasing incident:--

"It happened unfortunately ... that Monsieur Nicolas,
a man of most amiable character, and the father of a large
family, had not been so provident as the rest of his countrymen
in securing his effects within the Fort, but had left them
in the town; consequently, upon Colonel Clive's first taking
possession of the place, they had all been plundered by our
common soldiers; and the poor gentleman and his family
were to all appearance ruined. The generous and humane
Captain Speke,[56] having heard of the hard fate of Monsieur
Nicolas, took care to represent it to the two admirals in all
its affecting circumstances, who immediately advanced the
sum of 1500 rupees each. Their example was followed by
the five captains of the squadron, who subscribed 5000
between them. Mr. Doidge added 800 more, and the same
sum was thrown in by another person who was a sincere well-wisher
to this unfortunate gentleman; so that a present of
9600 rupees, or L1200 sterling was in a few minutes collected
towards the relief of this valuable Frenchman and his
distressed family. One of the company was presently
despatched with this money, who had orders to acquaint
Monsieur Nicolas that a few of his English friends desired
his acceptance of it, as a small testimony of the very high
esteem they had for his moral character, and of their
unfeigned sympathy with him in his misfortunes. The poor
gentleman, quite transported by such an instance of generosity
in an enemy, cried out in a sort of ecstasy, 'Good God,
they axe friends indeed!' He accepted of the present with
great thankfulness, and desired that his most grateful
acknowledgements might be made to his unknown benefactors,
for whose happiness and the happiness of their
families, not only his, but the prayers of his children's

children, he hoped, would frequently be presented to heaven.
He could add no more; the tears, which ran plentifully down
his cheeks, bespoke the feelings of his heart: and, indeed,
implied much more than even Cicero with all his powers of
oratory could possibly have expressed."

This, however, was but a solitary instance; the state of the French
was, as a rule, wretched in the extreme, and Renault wrote:--

"The whole colony is dispersed, and the inhabitants are
seeking an asylum, some--the greatest part--have gone to
Chinsurah, others to the Danes and to Calcutta. This
dispersion being caused by the misery to which our countrymen
are reduced, their poverty, which I cannot relieve,
draws tears from my eyes, the more bitter that I have seen
them risk their lives so generously for the interests of the
Company, and of our nation."

In such circumstances there was but one consolation possible to
brave men--the knowledge that, in the eyes of friend and foe, they
had done their duty. The officers of the British army and navy all
spoke warmly of the gallant behaviour of the French, and the
historian Broome, himself a soldier and the chronicler of many a
brave deed, expresses himself as follows:--

"The conduct of the French on this occasion was most
creditable and well worthy the acknowledged gallantry of
that nation. Monsieur Renault, the Governor, displayed
great courage and determination: but the chief merit of the
defence was due to Monsieur Devignes" (Captain de la
Vigne Buisson), "commander of the French Company's ship,
Saint Contest. He took charge of the bastions, and directed
their fire with great skill and judgment, and by his own

example inspired energy and courage into all those around
him."

Renault himself found some consolation in the gallant behaviour of
his sons.

"In my misfortune I have had the satisfaction to see my
two sons distinguish themselves in the siege with all the
courage and intrepidity which I could desire. The elder
brother was in the Company's service, and served as a
volunteer; the younger, an officer in the army, was, as has
been said above, commandant of the volunteers."

Others who are mentioned by Renault and his companions as having
distinguished themselves on the French side, were the Councillors
MM. Caillot, Nicolas, and Picques, Captain de la Vigne Buisson and
his son and officers, M. Sinfray (secretary to the Council), the
officers De Kalli[57] and Launay, the Company's servants Matel, Le
Conte Dompierre, Boissemont and Renault de St. Germain, the private
inhabitant Renault de la Fuye, and the two supercargoes of Indiamen
Delabar and Chambon. Caillot (or Caillaud) was wounded. The
official report of the loss of Chandernagore was drawn up on the
29th of March, 1757. The original is in the French Archives, and
Caillaud's signature shows that he was still suffering from his
wound. Sinfray we shall come across again. He joined Law at
Cossimbazar and accompanied him on his first retreat to Patna. Sent
back by Law, he joined Siraj-ud-daula, and commanded the small
French contingent at Plassey. When the battle was lost he took
refuge in Birbhum, was arrested by the Raja, and handed over to the
English.

The immediate gain to the English by the capture of Chandernagore
was immense. Clive wrote to the Select Committee at Madras:--

"I cannot at present give you an account to what value
has been taken;[58] the French Company had no great stock
of merchandize remaining, having sold off most of their
Imports and even their investment for Europe to pay in part
the large debts they had contracted. With respect to the
artillery and ammunition ... they were not indifferently
furnished: there is likewise a very fine marine arsenal well
stocked. In short nothing could have happened more
seasonable for the expeditious re-establishment of Calcutta
than the reduction of Charnagore" (i.e. Chandernagore). "It
was certainly a large, rich and thriving colony, and the loss
of it is an inexpressible blow to the French Company."[59]

The French gentlemen, after having signed under protest the document
presented to them by Clive, betook themselves to Chinsurah, where
they repudiated their signatures as having been extorted by force,
subsequent to, and contrary to, the capitulation. They proceeded to
communicate with Pondicherry, their up-country Factories, and the
native Government; they also gave assistance to French soldiers who
had escaped from Chandernagore. Clive and the Calcutta Council were
equally determined to interpret the capitulation in their own way,
and sent Renault an order, through M. Bisdom, the Dutch Director, to
repair to the British camp. Renault refused, and when Clive sent a
party of sepoys for him and the other councillors, they appealed to
M. Bisdom for the protection of the Dutch flag. M. Bisdom informed
them somewhat curtly that they had come to him without his
invitation, that he had no intention of taking any part in their
quarrels, that he would not give them the protection of his flag to
enable them to intrigue against the English, and, in short,
requested them to leave Dutch territory. As it was evident that the
British were prepared to use force, Renault and the Council gave in,
and were taken to Calcutta, where, for some time, they were kept
close prisoners. It was not till the Nawab had been overthrown at

Plassey, that they were absolutely released, and even then it was
only that they might prepare for their departure from Bengal.
Renault surmises, quite correctly, that this severity was probably
due to the fear that they would assist the Nawab.

The following incident during Renault's captivity shows how little
could be expected from the Nawab towards a friend who was no longer
able to be of use to him. After the capture of Chandernagore the
English Council called on the Nawab to surrender the French
up-country Factories to them. Siraj-ud-daula had not even yet
learned the folly of his double policy. On the 4th of April he wrote
to Clive:--

"I received your letter and observe what you desire in
regard to the French factories and other goods. I address
you seeing you are a man of wisdom and knowledge, and
well acquainted with the customs and trade of the world;
and you must know that the French by the permission and
phirmaund[60] of the King[61] have built them several factories,
and carried on their trade in this kingdom. I cannot
therefore without hurting my character and exposing
myself to trouble hereafter, deliver up their factories and
goods, unless I have a written order from them for so doing,
and I am perswaded that from your friendship for me you
would never be glad at anything whereby my fame would
suffer; as I on my part am ever desirous of promoting" [yours].

"Mr. Renault, the French. Governor being in your power, if
you could get from him a paper under his own hand and
seal to this purpose; 'That of his own will and pleasure, he
thereby gave up to the English Company's servants, and
empowered them to receive all the factories, money and
goods belonging to the French Company without any hindrance

from the Nawab's people;' and would send this to
me, I should be secured by that from any trouble hereafter
on this account. But it is absolutely necessary you come
to some agreement about the King's duties arising from the
French trade.... I shall then be able to answer to his
servants 'that in order to make good the duties accruing
from the French trade I had delivered up their factories
into the hands of the English.'"[62]

Clive replied on the 8th of April:--

"Now that I have granted terms to Mr. Renault, and
that he is under my protection, it is contrary to our custom,
after this, to use violence; and without it how would he ever
of his own will and pleasure, write to desire you to deliver
up his master's property. Weigh the justice of this in your
own mind. Notwithstanding we have reduced the French
so low you, contrary to your own interest and the treaty
you have made with us, that my enemies should be yours,
you still support and encourage them. But should you
think it would hurt your character to deliver up the French
factories and goods, your Excellency need only signify to me
your approbation and I will march up and take them."[63]

The more we study the records of the time, the more clearly we
realize the terrible determination of Clive's character, and we
almost feel a kind of pity for the weak creatures who found
themselves opposed to him, until we come across incidents like the
above, which show the depths of meanness to which they were prepared
to descend.

As to Renault's further career little is known, and that little we
should be glad to forget. Placed in charge of the French Settlement

at Karical, he surrendered, on the 5th of April, 1760, to what was undoubtedly an overwhelming British force, but after so poor a defence that he was brought before a Court Martial and cashiered. It speaks highly for the respect in which he had been held by both nations that none of the various reports and accounts of the siege mention him by name. Even Lally, who hated the French Civilians, though he says he deserved death,[64] only refers to him indirectly as being the same officer of the Company who had surrendered Chandernagore to Clive.

We shall now pass to what went on in Siraj-ud-daula's Court and capital.

NOTES:

[12: Journal of M. d'Albert.]

[13: Evidently the Parish Church of St. Louis. Eyre Coote tells us the French had four guns mounted on its roof.]

[14: In early accounts of India the Muhammadans are always called **Moors**; the Hindus, **Gentoos** or **Gentiles**. The **Topasses** were Portuguese half-castes, generally employed, even by native princes, as gunners.]

[15: Captain Broome says there were fifty European ladies in the Fort. The French accounts say they all retired, previous to the siege, to Chinsurah and Serampore.]

[16: Captain, afterwards Sir, Eyre Coote.]

[17: The fullest account is one by Renault, dated October

26, 1758.]

[18: The only one, excepting the battle of Biderra, between the English and Dutch.]

[19: Governor of Pondicherry and President of the Superior Council.]

[20: Eyre Coote, in his "Journal," mentions an old ditch, which surrounded the settlement.]

[21: One hundred toises, or 600 feet; but Eyre Coote says 330 yards, the difference probably due to the measurement excluding or including the outworks.]

[22: Tanks, or artificial ponds, in Bengal are often of great size. I have seen some a quarter of a mile long.]

[23: Letter to M. de Montorcin, Chandernagore, August 1 1756. Signature lost.]

[24: The Nawab, in July, 1756, extorted three lakhs from the French and even more from the Dutch.]

[25: British Museum. Additional MS. 20,914.]

[26: A kind of fibre used in making bags and other coarse materials.]

[27: Surgeon Ives's Journal.]

[28: Letter to De Montorcin.]

[29: Both English and French use this word "inhabitant" to signify any resident who was not official, military, or in the seafaring way.]

[30: This he did through the Armenian Coja Wajid, a wealthy merchant of Hugli, who advised the Nawab on European affairs. ***Letter from Coja Wajid to Clive, January 17, 1757.***]

[31: A French doctor, who has left an account of the Revolutions in Bengal, says there were eight outposts, and that the loss of one would have involved the loss of all the others, as they could be immediately cut off from the Fort, from which they were too distant to be easily reinforced. The doctor does not sign his name, but he was probably one of the six I mentioned above. Their names were Haillet (doctor), La Haye (surgeon-major), Du Cap (second), Du Pre (third), Droguet (fourth), and St. Didier (assistant).]

[32: M. Vernet, the Dutch Chief at Cossimbazar, wrote to the Dutch Director at Chinsurah that he could obtain a copy of this treaty from the Nawab's secretaries, if he wished for it.]

[33: See page 79 (and note).]

[34: See note, p. 89.]

[35: Governor.]

[36: A document authorising the free transit of certain goods, and their exemption from custom dues, in favour of English traders.-- ***Wilson***.]

[37: Orme MSS. India XI., p. 2744, No. 71.]

[38: Orme MSS. India XI., p. 2750, No. 83.]

[39: Still visible, I believe, in parts. The gateway certainly exists.]

[40: Mr. Tooke was a Company's servant. He had distinguished himself in the defence of Calcutta in 1756, when he was wounded, and, being taken on board the ships, escaped the dreadful ordeal of the Black Hole.]

[41: Neither of these accounts agree with the Capitulation Returns.]

[42: British Museum. Addl. MS. 20,914.]

[43: Remarks on board His Majesty's ship *Tyger*, March 15th.]

[44: His maternal grandfather was a cousin of Aliverdi Khan.]

[45: Malleson explains this by saying that De Terraneau was employed in the blocking up of the passage, but the story hardly needs contradiction.]

[46: This announcement seems superfluous after fighting had been going on for several days, but it simply shows the friction between the naval and military services.]

[47: Clive's journal for March 16th. Fort St. George, Sel. Com. Cons., 28th April, 1757.]

[48: Eyre Coote's journal.]

[49: The passages interpolated are on the authority of a
MS. in the Orme Papers, entitled "News from Bengal."]

[50: Accounts of this detail differ. One says it was
stormed on the 21st, but if so the French would have been more on
their guard, and would surely have strengthened the second battery
in front of the Fort.]

[51: Lime plaster made extremely hard.]

[52: The Emperor at Delhi, who was supposed to be about to
invade Bengal.]

[53: Orme MSS. O.V. 32, p. 11.]

[54: Orme MSS. O.V. 32, p. 10.]

[55: Sergeant Nover was pardoned in consideration of
previous good conduct. Letter from Clive to Colonel Adlercron,
March 29, 1757.]

[56: Captain Speke was seriously and his son mortally
wounded in the attack on Chandernagore.]

[57: I cannot identify this name in the Capitulation
Returns. Possibly he was killed.]

[58: Surgeon Ives says the booty taken was valued at
L130,000.]

[59: Orme MSS. India X., p. 2390. Letter of 30th March,
1757.]

[60: ***Firman***, or Imperial Charter.]

[61: The Mogul, Emperor, or King of Delhi, to whom the Bengal Nawabs were nominally tributary.]

[62: Orme MSS. India XI. pp. 2766-7, No. 111.]

[63: Ibid., p. 2768, No. 112.]

[64: Memoirs of Lally. London, 1766.]

CHAPTER III
M. LAW, CHIEF OF COSSIMBAZAR

A few miles out of Murshidabad, capital of the Nawabs of Bengal
since 1704, when Murshid Kuli Khan transferred his residence from
Dacca to the ancient town of Muxadabad and renamed it after himself,
lay a group of European Factories in the village or suburb of
Cossimbazar.[65] Of these, one only, the English, was fortified; the
others, i.e. the French and Dutch, were merely large houses lying in
enclosures, the walls of which might keep out cattle and wild
animals and even thieves, but were useless as fortifications. In
1756 the Chief of the English Factory, as we have already seen, was
the Worshipful Mr. William Watts; the Dutch factory was under M.
Vernet,[66] and the French under M. Jean Law. The last mentioned was
the elder son of William Law, brother of John Law the financier,
who settled in France, and placed his sons in the French service.
French writers[67] on genealogy have hopelessly mixed up
the two brothers, Jean and Jacques Francois. Both came to
India, both distinguished themselves, both rose to the rank of
colonel, one by his services to the French East India Company, and
one by the usual promotion of an officer in the King's army. The
only proof that the elder was the Chief of Cossimbazar is to be
found in a few letters, mostly copies, in which his name is given as
Jean or John. As a usual rule he signed himself in the French manner
by his surname only, or as Law of Lauriston.

His experiences during the four years following the accession of Siraj-ud-daula were painful and exciting, and he has recorded them in a journal or memoir[68] which has never yet been published, but which is of great interest to the student of Indian history. For us it has the added charm of containing a picture of ourselves painted by one who, though a foreigner by education, was enabled by his birth to understand our national peculiarities. In the present chapter I shall limit myself almost entirely to quotations from this memoir.

Law was by no means an admirer of Aliverdi Khan's successor,--

"Siraj-ud-daula, a young man of twenty-four or twenty-five,[69] very common in appearance. Before the death of Aliverdi Khan the character of Siraj-ud-daula was reported to be one of the worst ever known. In fact, he had distinguished himself not only by all sorts of debauchery, but by a revolting cruelty. The Hindu women are accustomed to bathe on the banks of the Ganges. Siraj-ud-daula, who was informed by his spies which of them were beautiful, sent his satellites in disguise in little boats to carry them off. He was often seen, in the season when the river overflows, causing the ferry boats to be upset or sunk in order to have the cruel pleasure of watching the terrified confusion of a hundred people at a time, men, women, and children, of whom many, not being able to swim, were sure to perish. When it became necessary to get rid of some great lord or minister, Siraj-ud-daula alone appeared in the business, Aliverdi Khan retiring to one of his houses or gardens outside the town, so that he might not hear the cries of the persons whom he was causing to be killed."

So bad was the reputation of this young prince, that many persons, among them Mr. Watts, imagined it impossible that the people would ever tolerate his accession. The European nations in Bengal had no regular representatives at the Court of the Nawab; and the Chiefs of the Factories at Cossimbazar, though now and then admitted to the *Durbar*, transacted their business mainly through *wakils*, or native agents, who, of course, had the advantage of knowing the language and, what was of much greater importance, understood all those indirect ways in which in Eastern countries one's own business is forwarded and that of one's rivals thwarted. Then, as now, the difficulty of dealing with native agents was to induce these agents to express their own opinions frankly and clearly.[70] So far from the English Chief being corrected by his *wakil*, we find the latter, whilst applying to other nobles for patronage and assistance, studiously refraining from making any application to Siraj-ud-daula when English business had to be transacted at Court.

The English went even further:--

"On certain occasions they refused him admission into their factory at Cossimbazar and their country houses, because, in fact, this excessively blustering and impertinent young man used to break the furniture, or, if it pleased his fancy, take it away. But Siraj-ud-daula was not the man to forget what he regarded as an insult. The day after the capture of the English fort at Cossimbazar, he was heard to say in full *Durbar*, 'Behold the English, formerly so proud that they did not wish to receive me in their houses!' In short, people knew, long before the death of Aliverdi Khan, that Siraj-ud-daula was hostile to the English."

With the French it was different:--

"On the other hand, he was very well disposed towards
us. It being our interest to humour him, we had received
him with a hundred times more politeness than he deserved.
By the advice of Rai Durlabh Ram and Mohan Lal, we had
recourse to him in important affairs. Consequently, we
gave him presents from time to time, and this confirmed his
friendship for us. The previous year (1755) had been a
very good one for him, owing to the business connected with
the settlement of the Danes in Bengal. In fact, it was by
his influence that I was enabled to conclude this affair, and
Aliverdi Khan allowed him to retain all the profit from it,
so I can say that I had no bad place in the heart of Siraj-ud-daula
It is true he was a profligate, but a profligate who
was to be feared, who could be useful to us, and who might
some day be a good man. Nawajis Muhammad Khan[71] had
been at least as vicious as Siraj-ud-daula, and yet he had
become the idol of the people."

Law, therefore, had cultivated the young Nawab. Mr. Watts, on the
other hand, was not only foolish enough to neglect him, but carried
his folly to extremes. He was not in a position to prevent his
accession, and ought therefore to have been careful by the
correctness of his behaviour to show no signs of being opposed to
it. So far from this, he is strongly suspected of having entered
into correspondence with the widow of Nawajis Khan, who had adopted
Siraj-ud-daula's younger brother[72] and was supporting his
candidature for the throne, and also with Saukat Jang, Nawab of
Purneah and cousin of Siraj-ud-daula, who was trying to obtain the
throne for himself. Still further, he advised Mr. Drake, Governor of
Calcutta, to give shelter to Kissendas, son of Raj Balav (Nawajis
Khan's *Diwan*), who had fled with the treasures in his charge when
his father was called to account for his master's property.

Contrary to Mr. Watts's expectations, Aliverdi Khan's last acts so smoothed the way for Siraj-ud-daula, and the latter acted with such decision and promptitude on his grandfather's death, that in an incredibly short time he had all his enemies at his feet, and was at leisure to attend to state business, and especially the affairs of the foreign Settlements. Aliverdi Khan had always been extremely jealous of allowing the European nations to erect any fortifications, but, during his last illness, all of them, expecting a contested succession, during which, owing to complications in Europe, they might find themselves at war with each other in India, began to repair their old walls or to erect new ones. This was exactly what Siraj-ud-daula wanted. His first care on his accession had been to make himself master of his grandfather's and uncle's treasures. To these he had added those of such of his grandfather's servants as he could readily lay hands on. Other wealthy nobles and officers had fled to the English, or were suspected of having secretly sent their treasures to Calcutta. It was also supposed that the European Settlements, and especially Calcutta, were filled with the riches accumulated by the foreigners. Whilst, therefore, the Nawab was determined to make all the European nations contribute largely in honour of his accession, and in atonement for their insolence in fortifying themselves without his permission, he had special reasons for beginning with the English. In the mean time, however, he had first to settle with his cousin, Saukat Jang, the Nawab of Purneah, so he contented himself with sending orders to the Chiefs of the Factories to pull down their new fortifications. Law acted wisely and promptly.

"I immediately drew up an *Arzi*, or Petition, and had one brought from the Council in Chandernagore of the same tenour as my own. These two papers were sent to Siraj-ud-daula, who appeared satisfied with them. He even wrote me in reply that he did not forbid our repairing old works, but merely our making new ones. Besides, the spies who had been sent to Chandernagore, being well received and satisfied with the presents made them, submitted a report favourable to us, so that our business was hushed up."

The English behaved very differently, and their answer, which was bold if not insolent in tone,[73] reached the Nawab at the very moment when he had received the submission of the Nawab of Purneah. Law adds:--

"I was assured that the Nawab of Purneah showed him some letters which he had received from the English. This is difficult to believe, but this is how the match took fire.

"Accordingly, no sooner had the Nawab heard the contents of the answer from the English, than he jumped up in anger, and, pulling out his sword, swore he would go and exterminate all the Feringhees.[74] At the same time he gave orders for the march of his army, and appointed several Jemadars[75] to command the advance guard. As in his first burst of rage he had used the general word Feringhees, which is applied to all Europeans, some friends whom I had in the army, and who did not know how our business had ended, sent to warn me to be on my guard, as our Factory would be besieged. The alarm was great with us, and with the English, at Cossimbazar. I spent more than twenty-four hours in much anxiety; carrying wood, provisions, etc., into the Factory, but I soon knew what to expect. I saw horsemen arrive and surround the English fort, and at the same time I received an official letter from the Nawab, telling me not to be anxious, and that he was as well pleased with us as he was ill pleased with the English."

Cossimbazar surrendered without firing a shot, owing to the treacherous advice of the Nawab's generals, and Siraj-ud-daula advanced on Calcutta. It was with the greatest difficulty that Law escaped being forced to march in his train.

"The remains of the respect which he had formerly felt for Europeans made him afraid of failure in his attack on Calcutta, which had been represented to him as a very strong place, defended by three or four thousand men. He wrote to me in the strongest terms to engage the Director of Chandernagore to give him what assistance he could in men and ammunition. 'Calcutta is yours,' he said to our agent in full *Durbar*; 'I give you that place and its dependencies as the price of the services you will render me. I know, besides, that the English are your enemies; you are always at war with them either in Europe or on the Coromandel Coast, so I can interpret your refusal only as a sign of the little interest you take in what concerns me. I am resolved to do you as much good as Salabat Jang[76] has done you in the Deccan, but if you refuse my friendship and the offers I make you, you will soon see me fall on you and cause you to experience the same treatment that I am now preparing for others in your favour.' He wished us to send down at once to Calcutta all the ships and other vessels which were at Chandernagore. After having thanked him for his favourable disposition towards us, I represented to him that we were not at war with the English, that what had happened on the Coromandel Coast was a particular affair which we had settled amicably, and that the English, in Bengal having given us no cause of offence, it was impossible for us, without orders either from Europe or Pondicherry, to give him the assistance he asked for. Such reasons could only excite irritation in the mind of a man of Siraj-ud-daula's

character. He swore he would have what he wanted
whether we wished it or not, and that, as we lived in his
country, his will ought to be law to us. I did my best to
appease him, but uselessly. At the moment of his departure
his sent us word by one of his uncles that he still counted
on our assistance, and he sent me a letter for the Governor of
Pondicherry, in which he begged him to give us the necessary
orders. I thought to myself this was so much time gained."

The Nawab captured Calcutta without any open assistance from the
French, and, though he set free most of the prisoners who survived
the Black Hole, he sent Holwell and three others before him to
Murshidabad. Law, who had already sheltered Mrs. Watts and her
family, and such of the English of Cossimbazar as had been able to
escape to him, now showed similar kindness to Holwell and his
companions. Of this he says modestly:--

"The gratitude Mr. Holwell expresses for a few little
services which I was able to render him makes me regret
my inability to do as much to deserve his gratitude as I
should have liked to do."[77]

He also, apparently with some difficulty, obtained consent to M.
Courtin's request for the release of the English prisoners at Dacca;
for--

"Siraj-ud-daula, being informed that there were two or
three very charming English ladies at Dacca, was strongly
tempted to adorn his harem with them."

Law's success in these matters is a striking instance of his
personal influence, for Siraj-ud-daula was by no means any longer
well disposed towards the French and Dutch.

"The fear of drawing on his back all the European nations at once had made him politic. At first he pretended to be satisfied with the reply sent by the Governor of Chandernagore, and assured him that he would always treat us with the greatest kindness. He said the same to the Dutch, but when Calcutta was taken the mask fell. He had nothing more to fear. Scarcely had he arrived at Hugli when he sent detachments to Chandernagore and Chinsurah to summon the commandants to pay contributions, or to resolve to see their flags taken away and their forts demolished. In short, we were forced to yield what the Nawab demanded; whilst he, as he said, was content with having punished a nation which had offended him, and with having put the others to ransom to pay for the expenses of the expedition. We saw the tyrant reappear in triumph at Murshidabad, little thinking of the punishment which Providence was preparing for his crimes, and to make which still more striking, he was yet to have some further successes."

It may be here pointed out that, not only did the Nawab not insist on the destruction of the French and Dutch fortifications, but he did not destroy the fortifications of Calcutta. This proves that if the English had shown the humility and readiness to contribute which he desired, he would have left them in peace at the first, or, after the capture of Calcutta, have permitted them to resettle there without farther disturbance. In short, the real necessity of making the European nations respect his authority, instead of guiding him in a settled course, merely provided a pretext for satisfying his greed. This is the opinion, not only of the French and English who were at Murshidabad when the troubles began, but of the English officials who went there later on and made careful inquiries amongst all classes of people in order to ascertain the real reason of

Siraj-ud-daula's attack upon the English.

His avarice was to prove the Nawab's ruin.

"Siraj-ud-daula was one of the richest Nawabs that had
ever reigned. Without mentioning his revenues, of which
he gave no account at the Court of Delhi, he possessed
immense wealth, both in gold and silver coin, and in jewels
and precious stones, which had been left by the preceding
three Nawabs. In spite of this he thought only of increasing
his wealth. If any extraordinary expense had to be met
he ordered contributions, and levied them with extreme
rigour. Having never known himself what it was to want
money, he supposed that, in due proportion, money was as
common with other people as with himself, and that the
Europeans especially were inexhaustible. His violence
towards them was partly due to this. In fact, from his
behaviour, one would have said his object was to ruin everybody.
He spared no one, not even his relatives, from whom
he took all the pensions and all the offices which they
had held in the time of Aliverdi Khan. Was it possible for
such a man to keep his throne? Those who did not know
him intimately, when they saw him victorious over his
enemies and confirmed as Nawab by a *firman*[78]from the
Great Mogul, were forced to suppose that there was in his
character some great virtue which balanced his vices and
counteracted their effects. However, this young giddy-pate
had no talent for government except that of making himself
feared, and, at the same time, passed for the most cowardly
of men. At first he had shown some regard for the officers of
the army, because, until he was recognized as Nawab, he felt
his need of them. He had even shown generosity, but this
quality, which was quite opposed to his real character, soon disappeared,

to make place for violence and greed, which decided
against him all those who had favoured his accession in the
hope that he would behave discreetly when he became Nawab."

Owing to the general disgust felt at Murshidabad for the Nawab, his
cousin, Saukat Jang, Nawab of Purneah, thought the opportunity
favourable for reviving his claims, and, early in October,
Siraj-ud-daula, hearing of his contemplated rebellion, invaded his
country.

"Every one longed for a change, and many flattered
themselves it would take place. In fact, it was the most
favourable opportunity to procure it. The result would have
been happiness and tranquillity for Bengal. Whilst contributing
to the general good--which even the Dutch might
have interested themselves in--we could have prevented
the misfortunes which have since happened to us. Three or
four hundred Europeans and a few sepoys would have done
the business. If we could have joined this force to the
enemies of Siraj-ud-daula we should have placed on the
throne another Nawab--not, indeed, one wholly to our taste,
but, not to worry about trifles, one to the liking of the house
of Jagat Seth,[79] and the chief Moors and Rajas. I am sure
such a Nawab would have kept his throne. The English
would have been re-established peaceably, they would certainly
have received some compensation, and would have had
to be satisfied whether they liked it or not. The neutrality of
the Ganges assured, at least to the same extent as in the time
of Aliverdi Khan, the English would have been prevented
from invading Bengal, and from sending thither the reinforcements
which had contributed so much to their success
on the Madras Coast. All this depended on us, but how
could we foresee the succession of events which has been as

contrary to us as it has been favourable to the English? As
it was, we remained quiet, and the rash valour of the young
Nawab of Purneah, whilst it delivered Siraj-ud-daula from
the only enemy he had to fear in the country, made it clear
to the whole of Bengal that the change so much desired
could be effected only by the English."

Mir Jafar and other leaders of the Nawab's army were about to
declare in favour of Saukat Jang when Ramnarain,[80] Naib of Patna,
arrived to support Siraj-ud-daula. Whilst the malcontents were
hesitating what to do, Saukat Jang made a rash attack on the Nawab's
army, and was shot dead in the fight.

"Behold him then, freed by this event from all his
inquietudes; detested, it is true, but feared even by those
who only knew him by name. In a country where predestination
has so much power over the mind, the star of
Siraj-ud-daula was, people said, predominant. Nothing could
resist him. He was himself persuaded of this. Sure of the
good fortune which protected him, he abandoned himself
more than ever to those passions which urged him to the
commission of every imaginable form of violence.

"It can be guessed what we had to suffer, we and the
Dutch, at Cossimbazar. Demand followed demand, and insult
followed insult, on the part of the native officers and soldiers;
for they, forming their behaviour on that of their master,
thought they could not sufficiently show their contempt for
everything European. We could not go outside of our Factories
without being exposed to annoyance of one kind or another."

Every one in the land turned wistful eyes towards the English, but
they lay inactive at Fulta, and it seemed as if help from Madras

would never come. The English, therefore, tried to bring about a revolution favourable to themselves at Murshidabad, and began to look for persons who might be induced to undertake it; but this was not easy, as the Moor nobles had little acquaintance with the Europeans. Of the Hindus in Bengal--

"the best informed were the bankers and merchants, who by their commercial correspondence had been in a position to learn many things. The house of Jagat Seth, for instance, was likely to help the English all the more because to its knowledge of them it joined several causes of complaint against Siraj-ud-daula. Up to the death of Aliverdi Khan it had always enjoyed the greatest respect. It was this family which had conducted almost all his financial business, and it may be said that it had long been the chief cause of all the revolutions in Bengal. But now things were much changed. Siraj-ud-daula, the most inconsiderate of men, never supposing that he would need the assistance of mere bankers, or that he could ever have any reason to fear them, never showed them the slightest politeness. He wanted their wealth, and some day or other it was certain he would seize it. These bankers, then, were the persons to serve the English. They could by themselves have formed a party, and, even without the assistance of any Europeans, have put another Nawab upon the throne and re-established the English, but this would have required much time. Business moves very slowly amongst Indians, and this would not have suited the English. The bankers also were Hindus, and of a race which does not like to risk danger. To stimulate them to action it was necessary for the English to commence operations and achieve some initial successes, and as yet there seemed no likelihood of their doing so. To negotiate with Siraj-ud-daula for a peaceful re-establishment was quite

as difficult, unless they were inclined to accept the very
hardest conditions, for the Nawab had now the most extravagant
contempt for all Europeans; a pair of slippers, he
said, is all that is needed to govern them."

Just as it seemed likely that the English would have to stoop to the
Nawab's terms, they received news of the despatch of reinforcements
from Madras. About the same time, it became known to both French and
English that France and England had declared war against each other
in the preceding May.[81] The English naturally said nothing about
it, and the French were too eager to see the Nawab well beaten to
put any unnecessary obstacles in their way. The negotiations with
the friends of the Europeans at Murshidabad were quietly continued
until Admiral Watson and Colonel Clive arrived. A rapid advance was
then made on Calcutta, which was captured with hardly any
resistance.

Siraj-ud-daula was so little disturbed by the recapture of Calcutta
that the French thought everything would terminate amicably, but,
possibly owing to the reputation of Watson and Clive, who had so
long fought against the French,[82] they thought it likely that, if
the English demanded compensation for their losses, the Nawab would
allow them to recoup themselves by seizing the French Settlements.
M. Renault, therefore, wrote to Law to make sure that, in any treaty
between the Nawab and the English, an article should be inserted
providing for the neutrality of the Ganges; but the French, at
present, were needlessly alarmed. The English had no intention of
creeping quietly back into the country. Watson and Clive addressed
haughty letters to the Nawab, demanding reparation for the wrongs
inflicted on the English; and the Admiral and the Council declared
war in the name of the King and the Company. This possibly amused
the Nawab, who took no notice of their letters; but it was a
different matter when a small English force sailed up the Hugli,

passed Chandernagore unopposed by the French, captured the fort of Hugli, burnt Hugli[83] and Bandel towns, and ravaged both banks of the river down to Calcutta. The French were in an awkward position. The English had passed Chandernagore without a salute, which was an unfriendly, if not a hostile act; whilst the Nawab thought that, as the French had not fired on them, they must be in alliance with them. Law had to bear the brunt of this suspicion. His common sense told him that the English would never consent to a neutrality, and he wrote to Renault that it was absolutely necessary to join the Moors.

> "The neutrality was by no means obligatory, as no treaty existed. In fact, what confidence could we have in a forced neutrality, which had been observed so long only out of fear of the Nawab, who for the general good of the country was unwilling to allow any act of hostility to be committed by the Europeans? Much more so when the English were at war with the Nawab himself. If they managed to get the better of him, what would become of this fear, the sole foundation of the neutrality?"

So Law wrote to Renault, begging him, if he could not persuade the English to sign a treaty of neutrality at once, to make up his mind and join the Nawab. We have seen why Renault could do neither, and Law, writing after the event says, generously enough:--

> "I am bound to respect the reasons which determined M. Renault as well as the gentlemen of the Council, who were all much too good citizens not to have kept constantly in their minds the welfare of our nation and the Company. People always do see things differently, and the event does not always prove the correctness or incorrectness of the reasons which have decided us to take one or the other course."

As soon as the Nawab heard of the plundering of Hugli he set out for Calcutta, but to blind the English he requested M. Renault to mediate between them. The English refusal to treat through the French had the effect of clearing up matters between the latter and the Nawab; but he could not understand why the French would not actively assist him. Certain, at any rate, that he had only the English to deal with, he foolishly played into their hands by marching to fight them on their own ground, whereas, if he had remained idle at a little distance, merely forbidding supplies to be sent them, he could have starved them out of Calcutta in a few months. As I have said before, Clive attacked his camp on the 5th of February, and so terrified him that he consented to a shameful peace, in which he forgot all mention of the neutrality of the Ganges. Law tells a curious story to the effect that what frightened the Nawab most of all was a letter from Admiral Watson, threatening to make him a prisoner and carry him to England. Watson's letter is extant, and contains no such threat, but it is quite possible that it was so interpreted to the Nawab.

Though the Nawab had assured the English that he would have the same friends and enemies as they, and had omitted to mention the French in the treaty, he now, of his own accord, gave the French all that the English had extorted from him. This act could not be kept secret.

"A great fault at present, and which has always existed, in the management of affairs in India, especially in Bengal, is that nothing is secret. Scarcely had the Nawab formed any project when it was known to the lowest of his slaves. The English, who were suspicious, and who had for friends every one who was an enemy of Siraj-ud-daula, whom all detested, were soon informed of his proposals to M. Renault and of the letters written on both sides."

Yet Law thinks it was only the European war and the fear that
Renault intended an alliance with the Nawab that induced the English
to proceed to extremities:--

"The dethronement of the Nawab had become an absolute
necessity. To drive us out of Bengal was only a preliminary
piece of work. A squadron of ours with considerable forces
might arrive. Siraj-ud-daula might join his forces to it.
What, then, would become of the English? They needed
for Nawab a man attached to their interests. Besides, this
revolution was not so difficult to carry out as one might
imagine. With Chandernagore destroyed, nothing could be
more easy; but even if we were left alone the revolution
could have been effected by the junction of the English with
the forces which would have been produced against Siraj-ud-daula
by the crowd of enemies whom he had, and amongst
whom were to be counted the most respectable persons in
the three provinces.[84] This statement demands an explanation.
I have already spoken of the house of Jagat Seth, or
rather of its chiefs, who are named Seth Mahtab Rai and Seth
Sarup Chand, bankers of the Mogul, the richest and most
powerful merchants who have ever lived. They are, I can
say, the *movers* of the revolution. Without them the English
would never have carried out what they have. I have
already said they were not pleased with Siraj-ud-daula, who
did not show them the same respect as the old Nawab
Aliverdi Khan had done; but the arrival of the English
forces, the capture of the Moorish forts, and the fright of
the Nawab before Calcutta, had made a change which was
apparently in their favour. The Nawab began to perceive
that the bankers were necessary to him. The English
would have no one except them as mediators, and so they
had become, as it were, responsible for the behaviour of

both the Nawab and the English. Accordingly after the Peace there was nothing but kindness and politeness from the Nawab towards them, and he consulted them in everything. At the bottom this behaviour of his was sheer trickery. The Seths were persuaded that the Nawab who hated the English must also dislike the persons whom the English employed. Profiting by the hatred which the Nawab had drawn on himself by his violence, and distributing money judiciously, they had long since gained over those who were nearest to the Nawab, whose imprudence always enabled them to know what he had in his heart. From what came to the knowledge of the Seths it was easy to guess what he intended, and this made them tremble, for it was nothing less than their destruction, which could be averted only by his own. The cause of the English had become that of the Seths; their interests were identical. Can one be surprised to see them acting in concert? Further, when one remembers that it was this same house of bankers that overthrew Sarfaraz Khan[85] to enthrone Aliverdi Khan, and who, during the reign of the latter, had the management of all important business, one must confess that it ought not to be difficult for persons of so much influence to execute a project in which, the English were taking a share."[86]

Law could not persuade Renault to act, and without his doing so the game was nearly hopeless. Still, he worked at forming a French party in the Court. By means of Coja Wajid, an Armenian merchant of Hugli, whose property had been plundered by the English, he obtained an interview with the Nawab, and persuaded him to send the 2000 soldiers who were with Renault at the beginning of the siege. More would have been despatched but for the apparent certainty that the treaty of neutrality would be signed. In fact, Renault was so worried that, on the complaint of Watson and Clive that Law was exciting the Nawab against the English, he wrote Law a letter which caused the latter to ask to be recalled from Cossimbazar, and it was only at Renault's earnest request that he consented to remain at his post. Law continued forming his party.

"It would appear from the English memoirs that we corrupted the whole **Durbar** at Murshidabad to our side by presents and lies. I might with justice retort this reproach. As a matter of fact, except Siraj-ud-daula himself, one may say the English had the whole **Durbar** always in their favour. Without insisting on this point, let us honestly agree, since the English themselves confess it, that we were, like them, much engaged in opposing corruption to corruption in order to gain the friendship of scoundrels so as to place ourselves on equal terms with our enemies. This has always happened, and ought not to cause surprise in a Court where right counts for nothing and, every other motive apart, one can never be successful except by the weight of what one puts in the balance of iniquity. For the rest, right or wrong, it is certain that the English were always in a position to put in more than we could.

"Fear and greed are the two chief motives of Indian minds. Everything depends on one or the other. Often they are combined towards the same object, but, when they are opposed, fear always conquers. A proof of this is easily to be seen in all the events connected with, the revolution in Bengal. When, in 1756, Siraj-ud-daula determined to expel the English, fear and greed combined to make him act. As soon as he had himself proved the superiority of the English troops, fear took the upper hand in his mind, grew stronger day by day, and soon put him in a condition in which he was unable to follow, and often even to see, his true interests.

"I mention the Nawab first. His hatred for the English certainly indicated friendship for us. I think so myself, but we have seen what was his character and his state of mind in general. I ask, in all good faith, whether we could expect any advantage from his friendship? This person, cowed by fear, irresolute and imprudent, could he alone be of any use to us? It was necessary for him to be supported by some one who had his confidence and was capable by his own firmness of fixing the irresolution of the Prince.

"Mohan Lal, chief *Diwan* of Siraj-ud-daula, was this man, the greatest scoundrel the earth has ever borne, worthy minister of such a master, and yet, in truth, the only person who was really attached to him. He had firmness and also sufficient judgment to understand that the ruin of Siraj-ud-daula must necessarily bring on his own. He was as much, detested as his master. The sworn enemy of the Seths, and capable of holding his own against them, I think those bankers would not have succeeded so easily in their project if he had been free to act, but, unfortunately for us, he had been for some time, and was at this most critical moment dangerously ill. He could not leave his house. I went to see him twice with Siraj-ud-daula, but it was not possible to get a word from him. There is strong reason to believe he had been poisoned. Owing to this, Siraj-ud-daula saw himself deprived of his only support.

"Coja Wajid, who had introduced me to the Nawab, and who, it would be natural to suppose, was our patron, was a great merchant of Hugli. He was consulted by the Nawab only because, as he had frequented the Europeans and especially

the English, the Nawab imagined he knew them perfectly.
He was one of the most timid of men, who wanted
to be polite to everybody, and who, had he seen the dagger
raised, would have thought he might offend Siraj-ud-daula
by warning him that some one intended to assassinate him.[87]
Possibly he did not love the Seths, but he feared them,
which was sufficient to make him useless to us.

"Rai Durlabh Ram, the other *Diwan* of the Nawab, was
the man to whom I was bound to trust most. Before the
arrival of Clive he might have been thought the enemy of
the English. It was he who pretended to have beaten them
and to have taken Calcutta. He wished, he said, to maintain
his reputation; but after the affair of the 5th of February,
in which the only part he took was to share in the flight, he
was not the same man; he feared nothing so much as to
have to fight the English. This fear disposed him to gradually
come to terms with the Seths, of whose greatness he
was very jealous. He also hated the Nawab, by whom he
had been ill-used on many occasions. In short, I could never
get him to say a single word in our favour in the *Durbar*.
The fear of compromising himself made him decide to remain
neutral for the present, though firmly resolved to join finally
the side which appeared to him to be the strongest."

This, then, was the French party, whose sole bond was dislike to the
Seths, and the members of which, by timidity or ill-health, were
unable to act. It was different with their enemies.

"The English had on their side in the *Durbar* the terror
of their arms, the faults of Siraj-ud-daula, the ruling influence
and the refined policy of the Seths, who, to conceal their game
more completely, and knowing that it pleased the Nawab,

often spoke all the ill they could think of about the English,
so as to excite him against them and at the same time gain
his confidence. The Nawab fell readily into the snare, and
said everything that came into his mind, thus enabling his
enemies to guard against all the evil which otherwise he
might have managed to do them. The English had also on
their side all the chief officers in the Nawab's army--Jafar
All Khan, Khodadad Khan Latty, and a number of others
who were attached to them by their presents or the influence
of the Seths, all the ministers of the old Court whom
Siraj-ud-daula had disgraced, nearly all the secretaries,[88] the
writers[89] of the **Durbar**, and even the eunuchs of the harem.
What might they not expect to achieve by the union of all
these forces when guided by so skilful a man as Mr. Watts?"

With such enemies to combat in the Court itself, Law heard that the
English were marching on Chandernagore. By the most painful efforts
he obtained orders for reinforcements to be sent to the French.
They--

"were ready to start, the soldiers had been paid, the Commandant[90]
waited only for final orders. I went to see him
and promised him a large sum if he succeeded in raising the
siege of Chandernagore. I also visited several of the chief
officers, to whom I promised rewards proportionate to their
rank. I represented to the Nawab that Chandernagore must
be certainly captured if the reinforcements did not set out
at once, and I tried to persuade him to give his orders to
the Commandant in my presence. 'All is ready,' replied the
Nawab, 'but before resorting to arms it is proper to try all
possible means to avoid a rupture, and all the more so as the
English have just promised to obey the orders I shall send
them.'[91] I recognized the hand of the Seths in these details.

They encouraged the Nawab in a false impression about this
affair. On the one hand, they assured him that the march
of the English, was only to frighten us into subscribing to
a treaty of neutrality, and on the other hand they increased
his natural timidity by exaggerating the force of the English
and by representing the risk he ran in assisting us with
reinforcements which would probably not prevent the capture
of Chandernagore if the English were determined to take it,
but would serve as a reason for the English to attack the
Nawab himself. They managed so well that they destroyed
in the evening all the effect I had produced in the morning.

"I resolved to visit the bankers. They immediately
commenced talking about our debts, and called my attention
to the want of punctuality in our payments. I said that
this was not the question just now, and that I came to them
upon a much more interesting matter, which, however, concerned
them as well as us with respect to those very debts
for which they were asking payment and security. I asked
why they supported the English against us. They denied it,
and, after much explanation, they promised to make any
suggestions I wished to the Nawab. They added that they
were quite sure the English would not attack us, and that
I might remain tranquil. Knowing that they were well
acquainted with the designs of the English, I told them I
knew as well as they did what these were, and that I saw
no way of preventing them from attacking Chandernagore
except by hastening the despatch of the reinforcements which
the Nawab had promised, and that as they were disposed to
serve me, I begged them to make the Nawab understand the
same. They replied that the Nawab wished to avoid any
rupture with the English, and they said many other things

which only showed me that, in spite of their good will, they
would do nothing for us. Ranjit Rai, who was their man
of business as well as the agent of the English, said to me
in a mocking tone, 'You are a Frenchman; are you afraid of
the English? If they attack you, defend yourselves! No
one is ignorant of what your nation has done on the Madras
Coast, and we are curious to see how you will come off in
this business here.' I told him I did not expect to find such
a warlike person in a Bengali merchant, and that sometimes
people repented of their curiosity. That was enough for such
a fellow, but I saw clearly that the laugh would not be on
my side. However, every one was very polite, and I left
the house."

Law thinks the Seths honestly believed that the English march on
Chandernagore was merely intended to frighten the French, and, as a
proof of their friendliness, narrates a further incident of this
visit:--

"The conversation having turned on Siraj-ud-daula, on
the reasons he had given the Seths to fear him, and on his
violent character, I said I understood clearly enough what
they meant, and that they certainly wanted to set up another
Nawab. The Seths, instead of denying this, contented themselves
with saying in a low voice that this was a subject
which should not be talked about. Omichand, the English
agent[92] (who, by the way, cried 'Away with them!' wherever
he went), was present. If the fact had been false, the Seths
would certainly have denied it, and would have reproached
me for talking in such a way. If they had even thought
I intended to thwart them, they would also have denied
it, but considering all that had happened, the vexations
caused us by the Nawab and our obstinate refusals to help

him, they imagined that we should be just as content as they were to see him deposed, provided only the English would leave us in peace. In fact, they did not as yet regard us as enemies."

Law was, however, ignorant that Clive had already promised, or did so soon after, to give the property of the French Company to the Seths in payment of the money the French owed them; but he now for the first time fully realized the gravity of the situation. The indiscretion of the Seths showed him the whole extent of the plot, and the same evening he told the Nawab, but--

"the poor young man began to laugh, not being able to imagine I could be so foolish as to indulge in such ideas."

And yet, whilst he refused to believe in the treason of his officers, the Nawab indulged at times in the most violent outbreaks of temper against them.

"Siraj-ud-daula was not master of himself.[93] It would have needed as much firmness in his character as there was deceitfulness to make the latter quality of use to him. At certain times his natural disposition overmastered him, especially when in his harem surrounded by his wives and servants, when he was accustomed to say openly all that was in his heart. Sometimes this happened to him in full *Durbar*."

The same evening, also, Mr. Watts came to the *Durbar*, and the matter of the neutrality was talked over. The Nawab wished the two gentlemen to pledge their respective nations to keep the peace, but Mr. Watts skilfully avoided giving any promise, and suggested the Nawab should write to the Admiral. Law, seeing that further delay

was aimed at, exclaimed that the Admiral would pay as little respect
to this letter as to the Nawab's previous ones.

"'How?' said the Nawab, looking angrily at me instead
of at Mr. Watts: 'who am I then?' All the members of his
Court cried out together that his orders would certainly be
attended to."

As Law expected, Chandernagore was attacked before the Admiral's
reply was received. Law received the news on the 15th, and hurried
to the Nawab. Reinforcements were ordered and counter-ordered. At
midnight the Nawab's eunuch came to inform Law that the English had
been repulsed with loss, and on the morning of the 16th the Nawab's
troops were ordered to advance, but when the same day news came that
the French had withdrawn into the Fort, every one cried out that the
Fort must fall, and that it was mere folly to incense the English by
sending down troops. They were immediately recalled. Then news
arrived that the Fort was holding out, and Rai Durlabh Ram was
ordered to advance. Again there came a false report that the Fort
had fallen. Law knew Rai Durlabh was a coward, and his whole
reliance was on the second in command, Mir Madan:--

"a capable officer, and one who would have attacked the
enemy with pleasure."

This Mir Madan is said to have been a Hindu convert to
Muhammadanism. Native poems still tell of the gallantry with which
he commanded the Hindu soldiers of the Nawab. He was one of the
first to fall at Plassey, and though it cannot be said that his
death caused the loss of the battle, it is certain that it put an
end to all chance of the victory being contested.

Law was at his wits' end. It was no time to stick at trifles, and, that he might know the worst at once, he intercepted Mr. Watts's letters. From them he gathered that the English intended to march straight upon Murshidabad. He set about fortifying the enclosure round the French Factory, and, as he had only 10 or 12 men, he induced the Nawab to send him a native officer with 100 musketeers. He soon learned that the reported English advance was merely the pursuit of the fugitives from Chandernagore, who were mentioned in the last chapter. By the end of March he had 60 Europeans:--

> "of whom the half, in truth, were not fit to serve; but what
> did that matter? The number was worth 120 to me outside
> the fort, since rumour always delights in exaggeration."

Of the sepoys also, whom the English set free, some 30 found their way to Law, and so far was he now from being afraid of Mr. Watts, that it was the latter who had to ask the Nawab's protection.

The vacillation which had marked the Nawab's conduct previous to the fall of Chandernagore still continued. He protected Law, but would not help him with money.

> "Further, at the solicitation of my enemies, the Nawab
> sent people to pull down the earthworks I had erected. He
> even wished the native agent of the English to be present.
> In my life I have never suffered what I did that day. To
> the orders of the Nawab I replied that so long as I was in
> the Factory no foreigner should touch my fortifications, but
> that to keep my agreement with him I was ready to withdraw
> and to make over the Factory to him, with which he
> could afterwards do as he liked, and for which I should hold
> him responsible. At the same time, I made my whole troop
> arm themselves, and, having had my munitions loaded on
> carts for several days previous, I prepared to depart with

the small amount of money which belonged to me and to a few other individuals. The Nawab's officer, seeing my resolution, and fearing to do anything which, might not be approved, postponed the execution of his orders, and informed the Nawab of what was happening. He replied that he absolutely forbade my leaving the Factory, and ordered the pioneers to be sent away; but at the same time he informed me that it was absolutely necessary for me to pull down the earthworks, that under the present circumstances he had himself to do many things contrary to his own wishes, that by refusing to obey I should draw the English upon him and upon us, that we could not defend ourselves and must therefore submit, that I should not be troubled any more, and that, finally, he would give me money enough to build in brick what I had wished to make in earth. I knew well the value of his promises, but I was forced to humour him. It did not suit me to abandon the Factory altogether, so I set my workmen to pull down what I had built, and the same night the work was finished."

The English now tried to win over the French soldiers, and had some success, for many of them were deserters from the British forces, and they quickly saw how precarious was the shelter which Law could afford them; but the Nawab could not be persuaded to force Law to surrender, and, though he agreed to leave the country, Law declared he would not do even that unless he received passports and money. On the 8th of April he received passports, and was promised that if he would go to Phulbari, near Patna, he should there receive all he wanted. He was allowed four or five days to make his preparations.

"I profited by this interval to persuade the only man who dared speak for us to got to action. This was the Nazir Dalal, a man of no importance, but at the same time a man

in whom the Nawab appeared to have some confidence. As
he was constantly at the Factory, I had opportunities of telling
him many things of particular interest to the Nawab, and I
believed that by politeness and presents I had brought him
over to our interests. A little later, however, I learned that
he received quite as much from the English as from us. He
told the Nawab all that he learned from me, *viz.* the views
of the English and of the Seths, and the risk he himself was
running, and he brought to his notice that the English were
steadily increasing their garrison at Cossimbazar by bringing
up soldiers who pretended they were deserters and wished to
pass over to the Trench. By this trick, indeed, many soldiers
had passed through the Moorish camp without being stopped.
There was also talk of an English fleet preparing to come up
and waiting only for the Nawab's permission. The Nazir
Dalal represented to him that the trading boats might be
loaded with ammunition, and that they ought to be strictly
searched, and the casks and barrels opened, as guns and
mortars might be found in them. The Nawab opened his
eyes at information of this kind, and promptly sent the Nazir
Dalal to tell me not to leave. This order came on the 10th
of April. I accordingly passed my garrison in review before
the Nawab's agent, and a statement showing the monthly
pay of each officer and soldier was sent to the Nawab, who
promised to pay them accordingly."

On the 12th of April Law received a sudden summons to attend the
Durbar the next day.

"After some reflection, I determined to obey. I thought
that by taking presents I could avoid the inconveniences I
feared, so I arranged to start early on the morning of the 13th
with five or six persons well armed. A slight rain detained

us till 10 o'clock. On leaving I told my people that M. Sinfray was their commandant, and ordered him, if I did not return by 2 o'clock, to send a detachment of forty men to meet me. We arrived at the Nawab's palace about midday. He had retired to his harem. We were taken into the Audience Hall, where they brought us a very bad dinner. The Nawab, they said, would soon come. However, 5 o'clock had struck and he had not yet dressed. During this wearisome interval I was visited by some of the *Diwans*, among others by the *Arzbegi.*[94] I asked him why the Nawab had called me. He replied with an appearance of sincerity that as the Nawab was constantly receiving complaints from the English, about the numerous garrison we had in our Factory, he had judged it proper to summon both Mr. Watts and myself in order to reconcile us, and that he hoped to arrange matters so that the English should have nothing to fear from us nor we from them. He added that the Nawab was quite satisfied with my behaviour, and wished me much good. At last the *Durbar* hour arrives. I am warned. I pass into a hall, where I find Mr. Watts and a number of *Diwans*. The agent of the Seths is present Compliments having passed, one of the *Diwans* asks me if I have anything particular to say to Mr. Watts. I answer that I have not. Thereupon Mr. Watts addresses me in English: 'The question is, sir, whether you are prepared to surrender your Factory to me and to go down to Calcutta with all your people. You will be well treated, and will be granted the same conditions as the gentlemen of Chandernagore. This is the Nawab's wish.' I reply I will do nothing of the kind, that I and all those with me are free, that if I am forced to leave Cossimbazar I will surrender the Factory to the Nawab, and to no one else. Mr. Watts, turning round to the *Diwans*, says excitedly, that it is impossible to do anything with me, and repeats to them word for word all that has passed between us.

"From that moment I saw clearly that the air of the
Court was not healthy for us. It was, however, necessary to
put a good face on matters. The *Arzbegi* and some others,
taking me aside, begged me to consider what I was doing in
refusing Mr. Watts's propositions, and said that as the Nawab
was determined to have a good understanding with the
English, he would force me to accept them. They then
asked what I intended to do. I said I intended to stay at
Cossimbazar and to oppose, to the utmost of my power, the
ambitious designs of the English. 'Well, well, what can
you do?' they replied. 'You are about a hundred Europeans;
the Nawab has no need of you; you will certainly be forced
to leave this place. It would be much better to accept the
terms offered you by Mr. Watts.' The same persons who had
begged me to do this then took Mr. Watts aside. I do not
know what they said to each other, but a quarter of an hour
after they went into the hall where the Nawab was.

"I was in the utmost impatience to know the result of
all these parleyings, so much the more as from some words
that had escaped them I had reason to think they intended
to arrest me.

"Fire or six minutes after Mr. Watts had gone to the
Nawab, the *Arzbegi*, accompanied by some officers and the
agents of the Seths and the English, came and told me aloud,
in the presence of some fifty persons of rank, that the Nawab
ordered me to submit myself entirely to what Mr. Watts
demanded. I told him I would not, and that it was
impossible for the Nawab to have given such an order.
I demanded to be presented to him. 'The Nawab,' they

said, 'does not wish to see you.' I replied, 'It was he who
summoned me; I will not go away till I have seen him.'
The *Arzbegi* saw I had no intention of giving way, and that
I was well supported, for at this very moment word was
brought of the arrival of our grenadiers, who had been
ordered to come and meet me. Disappointed at not seeing
me appear, they had advanced to the very gates of the palace.
The *Arzbegi*, not knowing what would be the result of this
affair, and wishing to get out of the scrape and to throw the
burden of it on to the Seths' agent, said to him, 'Do you
speak, then; this affair concerns you more than us.' The
Seths' agent wished to speak, but I did not give him time.
I said I would not listen to him, that I did not recognize
him as having any authority, and that I had no business
at all with him. Thereupon the *Arzbegi* went back to the
Nawab and told him I would not listen to reason, and that
I demanded to speak to him. 'Well, let him come,' said
the Nawab, 'but he must come alone.' At the same time
he asked Mr. Watts to withdraw and wait for him in a
cabinet. The order to appear being given me, I wish to
go--another difficulty! The officers with me do not wish to
let me go alone! A great debate between them and the
Nawab's officers! At last, giving way to my entreaties,
and on my assuring them that I have no fears, I persuade
them to be quiet and to let me go.

"I presented myself before the Nawab, who returned my
salute in a kindly manner. As soon as I was seated, he told
me, in a shamefaced way, that I must either accept Mr.
Watts's proposals, or must certainly leave his territories.
Your nation is the cause, he said, of all the importunities I
now suffer from the English. I do not wish to put the whole country
in trouble for your sake. You are not strong enough to defend

yourselves; you must give way. You ought to remember that when I had need of your assistance you always refused it. You ought not to expect assistance from me now.

"It must be confessed that, after all our behaviour to him, I had not much to reply. I noticed, however, that the Nawab kept his eyes cast down, and that it was, as it were, against his will that he paid me this compliment. I told him I should be dishonoured if I accepted Mr. Watts's proposals, but that as he was absolutely determined to expel us from his country, I was ready to withdraw, and that as soon as I had the necessary passports I would go towards Patna. At this every one in concert, except the Nawab and Coja Wajid, cried out that I could not take that road, that the Nawab would not consent to it. I asked what road they wished me to take. They said I must go towards Midnapur or Cuttack. I answered that the English might at any moment march in that direction and fall upon me. They replied I must get out of the difficulty as best I could. The Nawab, meanwhile, kept his face bent down, listening attentively, but saying nothing. Wishing to force him to speak, I asked if it was his intention to cause me to fall into the hands of my enemies? 'No, no,' replied the Nawab, 'take what road you please, and may God conduct you.' I stood up and thanked him, received the betel,[95] and went out."

Gholam Husain Khan says that the Nawab was much affected at parting with Law, as he now believed in the truth of his warnings against the English and the English party,--

"but as he did not dare to keep him in his service for fear of offending the English, he told him that at present it was fit that he should depart; but that if anything new should

happen he would send for him again. '***Send for me again?***'
answered Law. 'Rest assured, my Lord Nawab, that this is
the last time we shall see each other. Remember my words: we
shall never meet again. It is nearly impossible."

Law hurried back to his Factory, and by the evening of the 15th of
April he was ready to depart. The same day the Nawab wrote to
Clive:--

"Mr. Law I have put out of the city, and have wrote
expressly to my Naib[96] at Patna to turn him and his attendants
out of the bounds of his Subaship, and that he shall not
suffer them to stay in any place within it."[97]

At the end of April the Nawab wrote to Abdulla Khan, the Afghan
general at Delhi, that he had supplied Law with Rs.10,000. Clive was
quickly informed of this.

On the morning of the 16th the French marched through Murshidabad
with colours flying and drums beating, prepared against any surprise
in the narrow streets of the city. Mr. Watts wrote to Clive:--

"They had 100 Europeans, 60 Tellingees, 30 ***hackerys***"
(i.e. bullock-waggons) "and 4 elephants with them."[98]

Close on their track followed two spies, sent by Mr. Watts to try
and seduce the French soldiers and sepoys. Law left a M. Bugros
behind in charge of the French Factory.

Shortly after leaving Cossimbazar, Law was reinforced by a party of
45 men, mostly sailors of the ***Saint Contest***, who had managed to
escape from the English. On the 2nd of May the French arrived at
Bhagulpur, the Nawab writing to them to move on whenever he heard

they were halting, and not to go so fast when he heard they were on the march.

> "To satisfy him we should have been always in motion
> and yet not advancing; this did not suit us. It was of the
> utmost importance to arrive at some place where I could
> find means for the equipment of my troop. We were
> destitute of everything."

These contradictory orders, and even letters of recall, reached Law on his march, but though he sent back M. Sinfray with letters to M. Bugros and Coja Wajid--which the latter afterwards made over to Clive--he continued his march to Patna, where he arrived on the 3rd of June, and was well received by Raja Ramnarain, and where he was within four or five days' march or sail from Sooty, the mouth of the Murshidabad or Cossimbazar river, and therefore in a position to join the Nawab whenever it might be necessary.

In the mean time fate had avenged Law on one of his lesser enemies. This was that Ranjit Rai, who had insulted him during his interview with the Seths. The latter had pursued their old policy of inciting the English to make extravagant demands which they at the same time urged the Nawab to refuse. To justify one such demand, the English produced a letter in the handwriting of Ranjit Rai, purporting to be written at the dictation of the Seths under instructions from the Nawab. The latter denied the instructions, and the Seths promptly asserted that the whole letter was a forgery of their agent's.

> "The notorious Ranjit Rai was driven in disgrace from
> the *Durbar*, banished, and assassinated on the road. It was
> said he had received 2 lakhs from the English to apply his
> masters' seal unknown to them. I can hardly believe this.
> This agent was attached to the English only because he knew

the Seths were devoted to them."

This incident warned the Seths to be more cautious, but still the plot against the Nawab was well known in the country. Renault, who had been at this time a prisoner in Calcutta, says:--

"Never was a conspiracy conducted as publicly and with such indiscretion as this was, both by the Moors and the English. Nothing else was talked about in all the English settlements, and whilst every place echoed with the noise of it, the Nawab, who had a number of spies, was ignorant of everything. Nothing can prove more clearly the general hatred which was felt towards him."[99]

M. Sinfray had returned to Murshidabad, but could not obtain an interview with the Nawab till the 8th of June, when he found him still absolutely tranquil; and even on the 10th the Nawab wrote to Law to have no fears on his account; but this letter did not reach Law till the 19th.

"I complained of the delay in the strongest terms to Ramnarain, who received the packets from the Nawab, but it was quite useless. The Nawab was betrayed by those whom he thought most attached to him. The Faujdar of Rajmehal used to stop all his messengers and detain them as long as he thought fit."

This officer was a brother of Mir Jafar.[100] The Seths and the English had long found the chief difficulty in their way to be the choice of a man of sufficient distinction to replace Siraj-ud-daula on the throne. At this moment the Nawab himself gave them as a leader Mir Jafar Ali Khan, who had married the sister of Aliverdi Khan, and was therefore a relative of his. Mir Jafar was *Bukshi*, or Paymaster and Generalissimo of the Army, and his influence had greatly contributed to Siraj-ud-daula's peaceful accession. He was a man of good reputation, and a brave and skilful soldier. It was such a person as this that the Nawab, after a long course of petty insults, saw fit to abuse in the vilest terms in full ***Durbar*** and to dismiss summarily from his post. He now listened to the proposals of the Seths, and towards the end of April terms were settled between him and the English.[101] The actual conclusion of the Treaty took place early in June, and on the 13th of that month Mr. Watts and the other English gentlemen at Cossimbazar escaped under the pretence of a hunting expedition and joined Clive in safety. As soon as he heard of this, the Nawab knew that war was inevitable, and it had come at a moment when he had disbanded half his army unpaid, and the other half was grumbling for arrears. Not only had he insulted Mir Jafar, but he had also managed to quarrel with Rai Durlabh. Instead of trying to postpone the conflict until he had crushed these two dangerous enemies, he begged them to be reconciled to him, and put himself in their hands. Letter after letter was sent to recall Law, but even the first, despatched on the 13th, did not reach Law till the 22nd, owing to the treachery of the Faujdar of Rajmehal. Law's letter entreating the Nawab to await his arrival certainly never reached him, and though Law had started at the first rumour of danger, before getting the Nawab's letter, he did not reach Rajmehal till the 1st of July. The Nawab had been captured in the neighbourhood a few hours before the arrival of his advance-guard. Gholam Husain Khan says that Law would have been in time had the Nawab's last remittance been a bill of exchange and not an order on the Treasury, for--

"as slowness of motion seems to be of etiquette with the people of Hindustan, the disbursing of the money took up so much time that when M. Law was come down as far Rajmehal, he found that all was over."

Law, who was nothing if not philosophical, remarked on this disappointment:--

"In saving Siraj-ud-daula we should have scored a great success, but possibly he would have been saved for a short time only. He would have found enemies and traitors wherever he might have presented himself in the countries supposed to be subject to him. No one would have acknowledged him. Forced by Mir Jafar and the English to flee to a foreign country, he would have been a burden to us rather than an assistance.

"In India no one knows what it is to stand by an unfortunate man. The first idea which suggests itself is to plunder him of the little[102] which remains to him. Besides, a character like that of Siraj-ud-daula could nowhere find a real friend."

Siraj-ud-daula, defeated by Clive at Plassey on the 23rd of June, was, says Scrafton,--

"himself one of the first that carried the news of his defeat to the capital, which he reached that night."

His wisest councillors urged him to surrender to Clive, but he thought this advice treacherous, and determined to flee towards Rajmehal. When nearly there he was recognized by a Fakir,[103] whose ears he had, some time before, ordered to be cut off. The Fakir informed the Faujdar, who seized him and sent him to Murshidabad, where Miran, Mir Jafar's son, put him to death on the 4th of July.

It was necessary for Law to withdraw as quickly as possible if he was to preserve his liberty. Clive and Mir Jafar wrote urgent letters to Ramnarain at Patna to stop him, but Ramnarain was no lover of Mir Jafar, and he was not yet acquainted with Clive, so he allowed him to pass. Law says:--

"On the 16th of July we arrived at Dinapur, eight miles above Patna, where I soon saw we had no time to lose. The Raja of Patna himself would not have troubled us much. By means of our boats we could have avoided him as we pleased, for though our fleet was in a very bad condition, still it could have held its own against the naval forces of Bengal, i.e. the Indian forces, but the English were advancing, commanded by Major Coote. As the English call themselves the masters of the aquatic element, it became us the less to wait for them, when we knew they had stronger and more numerous boats than we had. Possibly we could have outsailed them, but we did not wish to give them the pleasure of seeing us flee. On the 18th instant an order from the Raja instructed me in the name of Mir Jafar to halt--no doubt to wait for the English--whilst another on his own part advised me to hurry off. Some small detachments of horsemen appeared along the bank, apparently to hinder us from getting provisions or to lay violent hands on the boatmen. On this we set sail, resolved to quit all the dependencies of Bengal. In spite of ourselves we had to halt at Chupra, twenty-two miles higher up, because our rowers refused to go further: prayers and threats all seemed useless. I thought the English had found some means to gain them over. The boats did not belong to us, but we should have had little scruple in seizing them had our Europeans known how to manage them. Unfortunately, they knew nothing about it. The boats in Bengal have no keel, and consequently do not carry sail well. So we lost two days in discussion with the boatmen, but at last, by doubling their pay, terms were made, and five days after, on the 25th of July, we arrived at Ghazipur, the first place of importance in the provinces of Suja-ud-daula, Viceroy of the Subahs of Oudh, Lucknow, and Allahabad."

Before Law left Rajmehal on his return to Patna, the Faujdar tried to stop him on pretence that Mir Jafar wished to reconcile him to the English. Law thought this unlikely, yet knowing the native proclivity for underhand intrigue, he wrote him a letter, but the answer which he received at Chupra was merely an order to surrender. Law says:--

"I had an idea that he might write to me in a quite different style, ***unknown to the English***. I knew the new Nawab, whom I met at the time I was soliciting reinforcements to raise the siege of Chandernagore. He had not then taken up the idea of making himself Nawab. He appeared to me a very intelligent man, and much inclined to do us service, pitying us greatly for having to work with a man so cowardly and undecided as Siraj-ud-daula."

Law thought his communication--

"was well calculated to excite in his mind sentiments favourable to us, but if it did, Mir Jafar let none of them appear. The Revolution was too recent and the influence of the English too great for him to risk the least correspondence with us."

From Clive, on the other hand, he received a letter,--

"such as became a general who, though an enemy, interested himself in our fate out of humanity, knowing by his own experience into what perils and fatigues we were going to throw ourselves when we left the European Settlements."

This letter, dated Murshidabad, July 9th, was as follows:--

"As the country people are now all become your enemies, and orders are gone everywhere to intercept your passage, and I myself have sent parties in quest of you, and orders are gone to Ramnarain, the Naib of Patna, to seize you if you pursue that road, you must be sensible if you fall into their hands you cannot expect to find them a generous enemy. If, therefore, you have any regard for the men under your command, I would recommend you to treat with us, from whom you may expect the most favourable terms in my power to grant."[104]

Law does not say much about the hardships of his flight; but Eyre Coote, who commanded the detachment which followed him, had the utmost difficulty in persuading his men to advance, and wrote to Clive that he had never known soldiers exposed to greater hardships. At Patna Eyre Coote seized the French Factory, where the Chief, M. de la Bretesche, was lying ill. The military and other Company's servants had gone on with Law, leaving in charge a person variously called M. Innocent and Innocent Jesus. He was not a Frenchman, but nevertheless he was sent down to Calcutta. From Patna Eyre Coote got as far as Chupra, only to find Law safe beyond the frontier at Ghazipur, and nothing left for him to do but to return.

From now on to January, 1761, Law was out of the reach of the English, living precariously on supplies sent from Bussy in the south, from his wife at Chinsurah, and from a secret store which M. de la Bretesche had established at Patna unknown to the English, and upon loans raised from wealthy natives, such as the Raja of

Bettiah. He believed all along that the French would soon make an effort to invade Bengal, where there was a large native party in their favour, and where he could assist them by creating a diversion in the north. I shall touch on his adventures very briefly.

His first halt was at Benares, which he reached on the 2nd of August, and where the Raja Bulwant Singh tried to wheedle and frighten him into surrendering his guns. He escaped out of his hands by sheer bluff, and went on to Chunargarh, where he received letters from Suja-ud-daula, Nawab of Oudh, a friend of Siraj-ud-daula's, whom he hoped to persuade into invading Bengal. On the 3rd of September he reached Allahabad, and here left his troop under the command of M. le Comte de Carryon, whilst he went on to Lucknow, the capital of Oudh.

It is only at this moment that Law bethinks him of describing his troop. It consisted of 175 Europeans and 100 sepoys drilled in European fashion. The officers were D'Hurvilliers, le Comte de Carryon (who had brought a detachment from Dacca before Law left Cossimbazar), Ensign Brayer (who had commanded the military at Patna), Ensign Jobard (who had escaped from Chandernagore), and Ensign Martin de la Case. He also entertained as officers MM. Debelleme (Captain of a French East Indiaman), Boissemont, and La Ville Martere, Company's servants (these three had all escaped from Chandernagore), Dangereux and Dubois (Company's servants stationed at Cossimbazar), Beinges (a Company's servant stationed at Patna), and two private gentlemen, Kerdizien and Gourbin. Besides these, MM. Anquetil du Perron,[105] La Rue, Desjoux, Villequain, Desbrosses, and Calve, served as volunteers. His chaplain was the Reverend Father Onofre, and he had two surgeons, Dubois and Le Page. The last two were probably the surgeons of Cossimbazar and Patna. He had also with him M. Lenoir, second of Patna, whose acquaintance with the language and the people was invaluable. Law seems to have been always able to recruit his sepoys, but he had no great opinion of them.

"In fact it may be said that the sepoy is a singular animal, especially until he has had time to acquire a proper sense of discipline. As soon as he has received his red jacket and his gun he thinks he is a different man. He looks upon himself as a European, and having a very high estimation of this qualification, he thinks he has the right to despise all the country people, whom he treats as Kaffirs and wretched negroes, though he is often just as black as they are. In every place I have been I have remarked that the inhabitants have less fear of the European soldier, who in his disorderly behaviour sometimes shows an amount of generosity which they would expect in vain from a sepoy."

Law has left the following description of Lucknow:--

"Lucknow, capital of the Subah[106] so called, is 160 miles north of Allahabad, on the other side of the Ganges, and about 44 miles from that river. The country is beautiful and of great fertility, but what can one expect from the best land without cultivation? It was particularly the fate of this province and of a large portion of Oudh to have been exhausted by the wars of Mansur Ali Khan.[107] That prince at his death left the Treasury empty and a quantity of debts. Suja-ud-daula, his successor, thought he could satisfy his creditors, all of them officers of the army, by giving them orders upon several of the large estates. This method was too slow for these military gentlemen. In a short time every officer had become the Farmer,[108] or rather the Tyrant, of the villages abandoned to him. Forcible executions quickly reimbursed him to an extent greater than his claim, but the country suffered. The ill-used inhabitants left it, and the land remained uncultivated. This might have been repaired. The good order established by Suja-ud-daula commenced to bring the inhabitants back when an evil, against which human prudence was powerless, achieved their total destruction. For two whole years clouds of locusts traversed the country regularly with the Monsoon,[109] and reduced the hopes of the cultivator to nothing. When two days from Lucknow, we ourselves saw the ravages committed by this insect. It was perfect weather; suddenly we saw the sky overcast; a darkness like that of a total eclipse spread itself abroad and lasted a good hour. In less than no time we saw the trees under which we were camped stripped of their leaves. The next day as we journeyed we saw that the same devastation had been produced for a distance of ten miles. The grass on the roads and every green thing in the fields were eaten away down to the roots. This recurrent plague had driven away the inhabitants, even those who had survived the exactions of the military. Towns and villages were abandoned; the small number of people who remained--I am speaking without exaggeration--only served to augment the horror of this solitude. We saw nothing but spectres.

"The state of the people of Lucknow city, the residence of the Nawab, was hardly better. The evil was perhaps less evident owing to the variety of objects, but from what one could see from time to time nature did not suffer less. The environs of the palace were covered with poor sick people lying in the middle of the roads, so that it was impossible for the Nawab to go out without causing his elephant to tread on the bodies of several of them, except when he had the patience to wait and have them cleared out of the way--an

act which would not accord with Oriental ideas of
grandeur. In spite of this there were few accidents. The
animal used to guide its footsteps so as to show it was
more friendly to human beings than men themselves
were."

At Lucknow Suja-ud-daula greeted him with a sympathetic interest,
which Law quaintly likens to that shown by Dido for Aeneas, but
money was not forthcoming, and Law soon found that Suja-ud-daula was
not on sufficiently good terms with the Mogul's[110] Vizir[111] at
Delhi to risk an attack on Bengal. On the 18th of October he
returned to Allahabad, with the intention of going to Delhi to see
what he could do with the Vizir, but as it might have been dangerous
to disclose his object, he pretended he was going to march south to
Bussy in the Deccan, and obtained a passport from the Maratha
general, Holkar. This took some time, and it was not till March,
1758, that he started for Delhi. He reached Farukhabad without
difficulty, and on the 21st entered the country of the Jats. On the
evening of the 23rd a barber, who came into their camp, warned the
French they would be attacked. The next day the Jats, to the number
of 20,000, attacked them on the march. The fight lasted the whole
day, and the French fired 6000 musket shots and 800 cannon. The
cannon-balls were made of clay moulded round a pebble, and were
found sufficiently effective in the level country.

Soon after they arrived at Delhi, only to find the Marathas masters
of the situation and in actual possession of the person of the
Shahzada, or Crown Prince.[112] The Prince was friendly, gave Law
money, and eagerly welcomed the idea of attacking Bengal, but he was
himself practically a prisoner. The Vizir, too, could do nothing,
and would give no money. The Marathas amused him with promises, and
tried to trap him into fighting their battles. No one seemed to know
anything about what had happened in Bengal. He spoke to several of

the chief men about the English.

"I felt sure that, after the Revolution in Bengal, they
would be the only subject of conversation in the capital. The
Revolution had made much noise, but it was ascribed entirely
to the Seths and to Rai Durlabh Ram. Clive's name was
well known. He was, they said, a great captain whom the
Seths had brought from very far at a great expense, to
deliver Bengal from the tyranny of Siraj-ud-daula, as Salabat
Jang had engaged M. Bussy to keep the Marathas in
order. Many of the principal persons even asked me what
country he came from. Others, mixing up all Europeans
together, thought that I was a deputy from Clive. It was
useless for me to say we were enemies, that it was the
English who had done everything in Bengal, that it was
they who governed and not Jafar Ali Khan, who was only
Nawab in name. No one would believe me. In fact, how
could one persuade people who had never seen a race of
men different from their own, that a body of two or three
thousand Europeans at the most was able to dictate the law
in a country as large as Bengal?"

Law could do nothing at Delhi, and it was only by bribing the
Maratha general that he obtained an escort through the Jat country
to Agra. Most of his soldiers were glad to be off, but about 60
Europeans deserted with their arms to Delhi, where the Vizir offered
them pay as high as 50 rupees a month. M. Jobard was nearly killed
by some of them when he tried to persuade them to return to duty,
but, a few months after, more than half rejoined Law.

From Agra, Law went to Chatrapur in Bundelkand, where apparently,
though he does not say so, he was in the service of the Raja
Indrapat. His stay lasted from the 10th of June, 1758, to February,

1759. In order to keep on good terms with the inhabitants, who were almost all Hindus, Law forbade his men to kill cattle or any of the sacred birds, or to borrow anything without his permission, and at the same time severely punished all disorderly behaviour. The people having never heard of Christians, thought the French must be a kind of Muhammadans, but they could not make out from what country they came. Seeing them drink a red wine of which they had a few bottles, they thought they were drinking blood, and were horrified, but the good behaviour of the men soon put them on friendly terms.

Early in 1759 the Shahzada at last invaded Bengal, and on the 5th of February Law marched to join him; but the invasion was badly managed, and was an absolute failure. On the 28th of May Law was back at Chatrapur. The only result of the invasion was that the lands of a number of Rajas in Bihar were plundered by Miran, son of Mir Jafar, and the English. These Rajas were all Hindus.

> "They had an understanding with Ramnarain. All these
> Rajas, of whom there is a great number in the dependencies
> of Bengal, united to each other by the same religion, mutually
> support each other as much as they can. They detest the
> Muhammadan Government, and if it had not been for the
> Seths, the famous bankers, with whom they have close
> connections, it is probable that after the Revolution in which
> Siraj-ud-daula was the victim, they would all have risen
> together to establish a Hindu Government, from which the
> English would not have obtained all the advantages they
> did from the Muhammadan."

In 1759 the Dutch risked a quarrel with the English. They refused, however, any assistance from Law, who, far away as he was, heard all about it. They were defeated at Biderra on the 25th of November. The effect of this was to reduce Bengal to such tranquillity that Clive considered it safe to visit England. The Shahzada, however, thought the opportunity a favourable one for another invasion, and on the 28th of February, 1760, Law again started to join him. Patna was besieged, and, according to Broome, was very nearly captured, owing to Law's skill and the courage of his Frenchmen. In fact, the French were on the ramparts, when Dr. Fullerton and the English sepoys arrived just in time to drive them back.[113]

The siege was raised, and the Prince's general, Kamgar Khan, led the army about the country with apparently no object but that of plunder. This suited the Marathas, but did not suit Law. On one occasion he was ordered with his own troops and a body of Marathas to capture the little fort of Soupy. The French stormed it at three o'clock in the morning, but found that the Marathas, who had carefully avoided the breach, had swarmed the walls, where there was no one to oppose them, and were carrying off the plunder.

"My chief occupation and that of the officers, for more than five hours during which we stayed in Soupy, was to keep our soldiers and sepoys from bayoneting the Marathas, who, without having incurred the least danger, had, by their cleverness and lightness, carried off more than twenty times as much as our own men, observing among themselves a kind of order in their plundering, very like that of monkeys when they strip a field."

In fact, Law had a personal altercation with the Maratha commander about a young and beautiful Hindu woman, whom the Maratha wished to seize, but whom Law was determined to restore unhurt to her relations, who lived in a village close by.

For the capture of the fort, Law received from the Shahzada various high-sounding titles and the right to have the royal music played before him; but as he could not afford to entertain the native musicians, he allowed the privilege to sleep.

In 1760 Mr. Vansittart assumed the Governorship of Bengal, and his first act was to complete the project begun by his predecessor, Mr. Holwell, namely, the dethronement of Mir Jafar. This was effected on the 20th of October, 1760; the ex-Nawab went quietly to Calcutta, and Mir Kasim reigned in his stead. The Shahzada had now become Emperor by the death of his father, and had assumed the title of Shah Alam. He was still hanging with his army round Patna, and Mir Kasim and the English determined to bring him to book. Kamgar Khan continued to lead the Imperial army aimlessly about the country, and in January, 1761, found himself near the town of Bihar. He had 35 to 40 thousand cavalry, maintained chiefly by plunder, but his only musketeers and artillery were those commanded by Law, i.e. 125 Europeans and 200 sepoys, with 18 guns of small calibre. The British commander, Major Carnac, had 650 Europeans and 5 to 6 thousand sepoys, with 12 guns. Mir Kasim had some 20,000 cavalry, and the same number of musketeers, all good troops, for "everybody was paid in the army of Kasim Ali Khan."[114]

On the 14th of January, scouts brought word of the approach of the English. The Emperor consulted Law, who advised a retreat, but he was not deficient in courage, and determined to fight. The next day was fought the battle of Suan.[115]

"At the dawn of day we heard that the enemy were on the march, and that they would quickly appear. No disposition of our army had yet been made by Kamgar Khan, who, in fact, troubled himself very little about the matter. It was at first decided to re-enter the camp, so I put my men as much as possible under shelter behind a bank, along which I placed my guns in what I thought the most useful

positions. About 6 or 7 o'clock the enemy were seen
advancing in good order, crossing a canal[116] full of mud and
water, the passage of which might have been easily contested
had we been ready soon enough; but everything was neglected.
For some time we thought the enemy were going
to encamp by the canal, but, seeing that they were still
advancing, the order was given to go and meet them. The
whole army was quickly out of the camp, divided into
several bodies of cavalry, at the head of which were, on their
elephants, the Emperor, the Generalissimo Kamgar Khan,
and other principal chiefs. Scarcely were we out of the camp
when we were halted to await the enemy, everything in the
greatest confusion; one could see no distinction between
right, left, and centre, nothing that had the appearance of
an army intending to attack or even to defend itself.

"An aide-de-camp brought me an order to march ahead
with all my troop, and to place myself in a position which
he pointed out, a good cannon-shot away. Abandoned to
ourselves we should have been exposed to all the fire of the
English, artillery and even to be outflanked by the enemy
and captured at the first attack. We advanced a few paces
in obedience to the order, but, seeing no one move to support
us, I suspected they wanted to get rid of us. I therefore
brought back my men to where I had first placed them, on
a line about 200 paces in front of the army.

"The enemy advanced steadily. The English at their
head with all their artillery were already within range of
our guns. They quickly placed their pieces in two batteries
to the right and left, and kept up a very lively cross fire.
In a very short time, having killed many men, elephants,
and horses--amongst others one of mine--they caused the

whole of the Prince's army to turn tail. Kamgar Khan, at
their head, fled as fast as he could, without leaving a single
person to support us. The enemy's fire, opposed to which
ours was but feeble, continued steadily. We were forced to
retire, and did so in good order, having had some soldiers
and sepoys killed and one gun dismounted, which we left on
the field of battle. We regained the village, which sheltered
us for a time. The enemy started in pursuit. Unluckily,
as we issued from the village, our guns traversing a hollow
road, we were stopped by ditches and channels full of mud,
in which the guns stuck fast. As I was trying to disengage
them the English reached us, and surrounded us so as to
cut off all retreat. Then I surrendered with 3 or 4 officers
and about 40 soldiers who were with me, and the guns. It
was about 4 o'clock in the afternoon of the 15th of January,
1761, a moment whose malign influence it was as it were
impossible to resist, since it was that of the surrender of
Pondicherry,[117] a place 300 leagues away from us."

Gholam Husain Khan has left a graphic description of this incident.

"Monsieur Law, with the small force and the artillery
which he could muster, bravely fought the English themselves,
and for some time he made a shift to withstand their
superiority. Their auxiliaries consisted of large bodies of
natives, commanded by Ramnarain and Raj Balav, but the
engagement was decided by the English, who fell with so
much effect upon the enemy that their onset could not be
withstood by either the Emperor or Kamgar Khan. The
latter, finding he could not resist, turned about and fled.
The Emperor, obliged to follow him, quitted the field of
battle, and the handful of troops that followed M. Law,
discouraged by this flight and tired of the wandering life

which they had hitherto led in his service, turned about
likewise and followed the Emperor. M. Law, finding himself
abandoned and alone, resolved not to turn his back. He
bestrode one of his guns and remained firm in that posture,
waiting the moment for his death. This being reported to
Major Carnac, he detached himself from his main body with
Captain Knox and some other officers, and he advanced to
the man on the gun, without taking with him either a guard
or any Telingas[118] at all. Being arrived near, this troop
alighted from their horses, and, pulling their caps from their
heads, they swept the air with them, as if to make him a
salam; and this salute being returned by M. Law in the
same manner, some parley followed in their own language.
The Major, after paying high encomiums to M. Law for his
perseverance, conduct, and bravery, added these words: 'You
have done everything that could be expected from a brave
man; and your name shall be undoubtedly transmitted to
posterity by the pen of history; now loosen your sword from
your loins, come amongst us, and abandon all thoughts of
contending with the English.' The other answered that, if
they would accept of his surrendering himself just as he was
he had no objection, but that as to surrendering himself with
the disgrace of being without his sword, it was a shame he
would never submit to, and that they might take his life if
they were not satisfied with that condition. The English
commanders, admiring his firmness, consented to his surrendering
himself in the manner he wished; after which
the Major, with his officers, shook hands with him in their
European manner, and every sentiment of enmity was instantly
dismissed on both sides. At the same time that
commander sent for his own *palky*, made him sit in it, and
he was sent to the camp. M. Law, unwilling to see or to be
seen, in that condition, shut up the curtains of the *palky* for

fear of being recognized by any of his friends at camp, but
yet some of his acquaintances, hearing of his having arrived,
went to him; these were Mir Abdulla and Mustapha Ali
Khan. The Major, who had excused him from appearing in
public, informed them that they could not see him for some
days, as he was too much vexed to receive any company.
Ahmed Khan Koreishi, who was an impertinent talker,
having come to look at him, thought to pay his court to
the English by joking on this man's defeat--a behaviour that
has nothing strange [in it] if we consider the times in which
we live and the company he was accustomed to frequent; and
it was in that notion of his, doubtless, that with much pertness
of voice and air he asked him this question: 'And Bibi
Lass,[119] where is she?' The Major and the officers present,
shocked at the impropriety of the question, reprimanded him
with a severe look and very severe expressions. 'This man,'
they said, 'has fought bravely, and deserves the attention
of all brave men; the impertinences which you have been
offering him may be customary amongst your friends and
your nation, but cannot be suffered in ours, who has it for
a standing rule never to offer an injury to a vanquished foe.'
Ahmed Khan, checked by this reprimand, held his tongue,
and did not answer a word. He tarried about one hour
more in his visit, and then went away much abashed; and
although he was a commander of importance, and one to
whom much honour had always been paid, no one did speak
to him any more, or made a show of standing up at his
departure. This reprimand did much honour to the English;
and it must be acknowledged, to the honour of those
strangers, that as their conduct in war and battle is worthy
of admiration, so, on the other hand, nothing is more modest
and more becoming than their behaviour to an enemy,
whether in the heat of action or in the pride of success and

victory. These people seem to act entirely according to the rules observed by our ancient commanders and our men of genius."

Gholam Husain Khan says the victory was decided by the English; the following quotation from Major Carnac's Letter to the Select Committee at Calcutta, dated the 17th of January, 1761, shows how the courage of the British forces saved them from a great disaster.

"It gives me particular pleasure to inform you that we have not lost a man in the action, but a few of the Nawab's troops who had got up near our rear suffered considerably from the explosion of one of the French tumbrils. It seems the enemy had lain a train to it in hopes of it's catching while our Europeans were storming the battery, but fortunately we were advanced two or three hundred yards in the pursuit before it had effect, and the whole shock was sustained by the foremost of the Nawab's troops who were blown up to the number of near four hundred, whereof seventy or eighty died on the spot."[120]

Law continues:--

"The next morning, as the English army started in pursuit of the Emperor Shah Alam, Major Carnac, from whom, I must mention in passing, I received all possible marks of attention and politeness, sent me to Patna, where in the English Chief, Mr. McGwire, I found an old friend, who treated me as I should certainly have treated him in like circumstances. I was in need of everything, and he let me want for nothing."

Thus ended Law's attempt to maintain the French party in Bengal. All

hopes of a French attack in force on Calcutta had long since
disappeared, and, under the circumstances, his capture was fortunate
for himself and his comrades. Most of the latter were gradually
picked up by the English. Law was sent to Calcutta, and left Bengal
in 1762. He was now only forty-two years of age. On his arrival in
France he found his services much appreciated by his countrymen, and
was made a Chevalier of the Royal and Military Order of St. Louis,
and a Colonel of Infantry. Later on he was appointed Commissary for
the King, Commandant of the French Nation in the East Indies, and
Governor of Pondicherry. Law's account of his adventures was
commenced at Paris in 1763.[121] There exist letters written by him
to the historian Robert Orme, dated as late as 1785, which show the
strong interest he always retained in the affairs of Bengal, where
with adequate resources he might have played a much more
distinguished part.

We have seen a town besieged by a foreign army; we have seen the
Court of a great Prince distracted by internal dissensions and
trembling at the approach of a too-powerful enemy, and now we shall
pass to the quiet retreats of rural Bengal, which even their
remoteness could not save from some share in the troubles of the
time. In those days, even more than at present, the rivers were the
great highways of the country, but it needs personal acquaintance
with them to enable us to realize the effect they produce upon the
mind of a European. As a rule comparatively shallow, in the dry
weather they pursue a narrow winding course in the middle of a sandy
waste, but in the Rains they fill their beds from side to side,
overtop the banks, and make the country for miles around a series of
great lakes, studded with heavily wooded islands. Amidst these one
can wander for days hardly seeing a single human being, and hearing
nothing but the rushing of the current and the weird cries of
water-birds; at other times the prow of one's boat will suddenly
push itself through overhanging branches into the very midst of a

populous village. At first all is strange and beautiful, but after a short time the feeling grows that every scene is a repetition; the banks, the trees, the villages, seem as if we have been looking at them for a thousand years, and the monotony presses wearily on mind and heart. It was in a country of this kind that Courtin and his little band of Frenchmen and natives evaded capture for nearly nine months, and it adds to our admiration for his character to see how his French gaiety of heart unites with his tenderness for his absent wife, not only to conceal the deadly monotony of his life in the river districts during the Rains, and the depressing and disheartening effect of the noxious climate in which he and his companions had to dwell, but also to make light of the imminent danger in which he stood from the unscrupulous human enemies by whom he was surrounded.

NOTES:

[65: From certain letters it appears that, strictly speaking, the English Factory alone was at Cossimbazar, the French being at Saidabad, and the Dutch at Calcapur. Both Saidabad and Calcapur were evidently close to Cossimbazar, if not parts of it.]

[66: George Lodewijk Vernet, Senior Merchant.]

[67: The historian Malleson also confuses the two brothers.]

[68: The best copy I have seen is that in the Manuscript Department of the British Museum.]

[69: Gholam Husain Khan says that Siraj-ud-daula was born in the year in which Aliverdi Khan obtained from the Emperor the *firman* for Bihar. This, according to Scrafton, was 1736, and the connection of his birth with this auspicious event was the prime cause of his grandfather's great reference for him.]

[70: See note, p. 88.]

[71: Uncle of Siraj-ud-daula, who died so shortly before the death of Aliverdi Khan, that it was supposed he was poisoned to ensure Siraj-ud-daula's accession.]

[72: Fazl-Kuli-Khan. *Scrafton*.]

[73: Law says; "The rumour ran that M. Drake replied to the messengers that, since the Nawab wished to fill up the Ditch, he agreed to it provided it was done with the heads of Moors. I do not believe he said so, but possibly some thoughtless young Englishman let slip those words, which, being heard by the messengers, were reported to the Nawab."]

[74: Europeans. Properly, Franks or Frenchmen. This term was generally applied by Europeans to the half-caste descendants of the Portuguese.]

[75: Captains or generals: a term of somewhat indefinite meaning.]

[76: In alliance with Salabat Jang, Bussy temporarily acquired a large territory for the French.]

[77: "After Mr. Law had given us a supply of clothes, linen, provisions, liquors, and cash, we left his Factory with grateful hearts and compliments." *Holwell*. Letter to Mr. Davis, February 28, 1757.]

[78: Imperial Charter.]

[79: For an explanation of the influence of the Seths, see pp. 84, 85, and note.]

[80: Ramnarain is an interesting character. He appears to have been one of the most faithful of the adherents of the house of Aliverdi Khan and on its extinction of the English connection. His gallantry in battle is referred to by Colonel Ironside. Asiatic Annual Register, 1800.]

[81: The official intimation reached Admiral Watson in January, 1757, but apparently not the formal orders from the Admiralty. See page 30.]

[82: In a letter to the Secret Committee, London, dated October 11, 1756, Clive writes: "I hope we shall be able to dispossess the French of Chandernagore." So it is evident that he came with this intention to Bengal.]

[83: Clive describes Hugli as "the second city in the kingdom." *Letter to Lord Hardwicke, Feb*. 23, 1757.]

[84: Bengal, Bihar, and Orissa.]

[85: Hearing that Seth Mahtab Rai was to marry a wonderfully beautiful woman, he forced the Seths to let him see the young lady. *Scrafton*.]

[86: "If one is to believe certain English writers, the Seths were an apparently insurmountable obstacle to the project because of the money we owed them, as if in their perilous position these bankers would not be inclined to sacrifice something to save the greater part. Besides, we shall see by what follows that they sacrificed nothing." ***Law***. The extraordinary influence of these people was due not so much to their dealings with the head of the State as to the fact that native princes generally make payments, not in cash, but in bonds. It therefore depends on the bankers what any man shall get for his bonds. In this way an official, even when paid by the State, may be ruined by the bankers, who are merely private persons.]

[87: "In India it is thought disrespectful to tell a great man distinctly the evil which is said of him. If an inferior knows that designs are formed against the life of his superior, he must use circumlocutions, and suggest the subject in vague terms and speak in enigmas. It is for the great man to divine what is meant. If he has not the wit, so much the worse for him. As a foreigner, I was naturally more bold and said what I thought to Siraj-ud-daula. Coja Wajid did not hesitate to blame me, so that for a long time I did not know what to think of him. This man finally fell a victim to his diplomacies, perhaps also to his imprudences. One gets tired of continual diplomacy, and what is good in the beginning of a business becomes in the end imprudence." ***Law***.]

[88: "Witness the letter written to the English Admiral Watson, by which it is pretended the Nawab authorized him to undertake the siege of Chandernagore. The English memoir" (by Luke Scrafton) "confesses it was a surprise, and that the Secretary must have been bribed to write it in a way suitable to the views of Mr. Watts. The Nawab never read the letters which he ordered to be written; besides, the Moors never sign their names; the envelope being closed and well fastened, the Secretary asks the Nawab for his seal, and seals it in his presence. Often there is a counterfeit seal." ***Law***. From this it may be seen that the Nawab could always assert that his Secretary had exceeded his instructions, whilst it was open to his correspondent to assert the contrary.]

[89: The clerks.]

[90: "This was the boaster Rai Durlabh Ram, who had already received much from me, but all the treasures of the Universe could not have freed him from the fear he felt at having to fight the English. He had with him as his second in command a good officer, Mir Madan, the only man I counted upon." *Law*.]

[91: Referring to Clive's letter of the 7th of March, saying he wished to attack Chandernagore, but would await the Nawab's orders at that place.]

[92: By "agent" Law must mean simply an agent in the plot.]

[93: Scrafton, in his "Reflections" (*pp. 40 and 50*), says, Siraj-ud-daula indulged in all sorts of debauchery; but his grandfather, in his last illness, made him swear on the Koran to give up drinking. He kept his oath, but probably his mind was affected by his previous excesses.]

[94: Arzbegi, i.e. the officer who receives petitions.]

[95: A preparation of betel-nut (areca-nut) is used by the natives of Hindustan as a digestive. When offered to a guest, it is a sign of welcome or dismissal. When sent by a messenger, it is an assurance of friendship and safe conduct.]

[96: The Governor of Patna was Raja Ramnarain, a Hindu, with the rank of Naib only. It was considered unsafe to entrust so important a post to a Muhammadan, or an officer with the rank of Nawab.]

[97: Orme MSS. India XI., p. 2779, No. 120.]

[98: Ibid., India IX., p. 2294.]

[99: Letter from Renault to Dupleix. Dated Chandernagore, Sept. 4, 1757.]

[100: Broome (p. 154) gives his name as Mir Daood.]

[101: The Council signed the Treaty with Mir Jafar on the 19th of May, but Mr. Watts's first intimation of his readiness to join the English is, I believe, in a letter dated the 26th of April. Mir Jafar signed the Treaty early in June.]

[102: So Suja-ud-daula, Nawab of Oudh, plundered the Nawab Mir Kasim, when the English drove him from Bengal in 1763.]

[103: Broome (p. 154) says "a fakier, named Dana Shah, whose nose and ears he had ordered to be cut off thirteen months before, when on his march against the Nawaub of Purneah."]

[104: Orme MSS., India Office, and Clive correspondence at Walcot, vol. iv.]

[105: The celebrated traveller. He quickly quarrelled with and left them.]

[106: Province.]

[107: Nawab of Oudh and father of Suja-ud-daula.]

[108: I.e. the receiver of the rent or revenue.]

[109: The regular winds of the various seasons are called monsoons, and are named after the point of the compass from which they blow.]

[110: Alamgir II.]

[111: Imad-ul-mulk, Ghazi-ud-din Khan.]

[112: Ali Gauhar, born 1728. On the death of his father, November 29, 1759, he assumed the name or title of Shah Alam.]

[113: The old English Factory at Patna was re-opened by Mr. Pearkes, in July, 1757. See his letters to Council, dated 12th and 14th July, 1757.]

[114: Kasim Ali had a much better army than any of his predecessors. Though it was not trained in the European manner, several of the chief officers were Armenians, who effected great reforms in discipline. Three years later it made a really good fight against the English.]

[115: The battle is generally known as that of Gaya, but was fought at Suan. The site is marked in Rennell's map of South Bihar. It lies about six miles west of the town of Bihar, on the river Banowra.]

[116: The Banowra River.]

[117: The French capital on the Madras coast. Surrendered to Eyre Coote.]

[118: Sepoys, so called from the Telingana district in Madras, where they were first recruited.]

[119: Mrs. Law. **Bibi** is the equivalent of mistress or
lady. **Lass** was the native version of Law. Mrs. Law's maiden name
was Jeanne Carvalho.]

[120: Bengal Select Com. Consultations, 28th January,
1761.]

[121: "A part of these Memoirs was written at Paris in
1703, and part at sea in 1764, during my second voyage to India, but
several of the notes were added later." **Law**.]

CHAPTER IV
M. COURTIN, CHIEF OF DACCA

Jacques Ignace, son of Francois Courtin, Chevalier, Seigneur de Nanteuil, and of Catherine Colin, is, I believe, the correct designation of the gentleman who appears in all the records of the French and English East India Companies as M. Courtin, Chief of the French Factory at Dacca.

In June 1756, when Siraj-uc-daula marched on Calcutta, he sent word to his representative, the Nawab Jusserat Khan at Dacca, to seize the English Factory, and make prisoners of the Company's servants and soldiers. The English Factory on the site of the present Government College, was--

> "little better than a common house, surrounded with a thin brick wall, one half of it not above nine foot high." The garrison consisted "of a lieutenant" (Lieutenant John Cudmore), "4 serjeants, 3 corporals, and 19 European soldiers, besides 34 black Christians[122] and 60 *Buxerries*."[123]

On the 27th of June Jusserat Khan sent on the Nawab's order by the English *wakil*, or agent, to Mr. Becher, the English Chief, and informed him of the capture of Fort William and the flight of Mr. Drake. Thinking this was merely a trick to frighten them into surrender, the Dacca Council requested Mr. Scrafton, third in

Council, to write to M. Courtin, chief of the French Factory, for information. In reply M. Courtin sent them a number of letters which he had received from Chandernagore, confirming the bad news from Calcutta. Taking into consideration the unfortified condition of the Factory, and that Dacca was only four days by river from Murshidabad whilst it was fourteen from Calcutta, it seemed idle to hope to defend it even when assistance could be expected from the latter place, and, now that it was certain that Calcutta itself had fallen, any attempt at defence appeared rather "an act of rashness than of bravery." It was therefore resolved to obtain the best terms they could through the French.

The next day M. Fleurin, second of the French Factory--M. Courtin[124] was not well acquainted with the English language--came to inform them that the Nawab of Dacca agreed that the ladies and gentlemen should be allowed to retire to the French Factory on M. Courtin giving his word that they would there await the orders of Siraj-ud-daula as to their future fate. The soldiers were to lay down their arms, and be prisoners to the Nawab. This amicable arrangement was entirely due to M. Courtin's good offices, and he was much congratulated on the tact he had shown in preventing the Nawab from using violent measures, as he seemed inclined to do at first. As the Nawab would not allow the English to take away any of their property, except the clothes they were wearing, they were entirely dependent upon the French for everything, and were treated with the greatest kindness. The Council wrote:--

"The French have behaved with the greatest humanity
to such as have taken refuge at their Factory, and the tenour
of their conduct everywhere to us on this melancholy occasion
has been such as to merit the grateful acknowledgment of
our nation."

For some two months the English remained in the French Factory, M. Law, at Cossimbazar, warmly soliciting their release from Siraj-ud-daula. This he obtained with difficulty, and at last Mr. Becher and his companions sailed in a sloop provided by M. Courtin for Fulta, where they arrived safely on the 26th of August. When Calcutta had been recaptured by the English, M. Courtin, like a good business man, sent in a bill for the costs of the sloop to the Council at Calcutta, and the Consultations of the 16th of May, 1757, duly notify its payment.

The English did not regain possession of the Factory at Dacca till the 8th of March, by which time the declaration of War between France and England was known, and the likelihood of troubles in Bengal was very apparent. As we have seen, the English were successful in their attack on Chandernagore, but the whole country was aware that the Nawab was only the more enraged with them, and his local officers might at any moment be instructed to take vengeance on Englishmen found defenceless up country. On the 23rd of March, Messrs. Sumner and Waller wrote from Dacca that Jusserat Khan had refused to restore the Factory cannon, and to pass their goods without a new *parwana*[125] from Murshidabad. It was therefore still very doubtful whether he would assist the English or the French at Dacca, and though the English obtained the *parwana* they wanted early in May, on the 9th the Council at Calcutta sent them orders to do the best they could for their own security, and informed them they had sent an armed sloop to Luckipore to cover their retreat. They immediately sent down all the goods they could, but as matters became quieter again they soon resumed business, and appear to have had no further trouble.

It may be imagined that M. Courtin and his friends, knowing that the English had demanded the surrender of the French Factories, had a very uncomfortable experience all this time.[126] Unfortunately no

Records of the French Factories in Bengal are now to be found, and I had despaired of obtaining any information about the expulsion from Dacca, when, in the Bibliotheque Nationale at Paris, I came on a MS. entitled, "Copy of a letter from M. Courtin from India, written to his wife, in which are given in detail the different affairs which he had with the Moors from the 22nd of June, 1757, the day of his evacuation of Dacca, to the 9th of March, 1758."[127]

M. Courtin had married a Madame Direy, widow of a French Company's servant, and the letter shows she was fortunately in France at the time of her husband's troubles. As was natural, but inconveniently enough for us, Courtin does not think it necessary to trouble her with unintelligible and unpronounceable Indian names. Where possible, I shall fill them in from the English Records, otherwise I shall interrupt the course of the letter as little as possible. It runs as follows:--

"Calcapur,[128] April 20, 1758.

"Word must have reached thee in France of the loss of Chandernagore, which was taken from us by the English on the 23rd of March, 1757, after eleven days' siege. I was then at Dacca, and expecting every day to see M. Chevalier return from his journey to the King of Assam. Judge, my dear wife, of the chagrin and embarrassment into which I was thrown by this deplorable event. The English had had no idea of attacking Chandernagore until they had recovered Calcutta from the Moors, taken the Moorish village at Hugli, and forced the Moors to agree to a most shameful peace. This was not, as thou wilt see, sufficient for them, for Siraj-ud-daula had offended them too deeply for them to stop when once they found themselves on a good road; but unfortunately we were an obstacle in the way of their

vengeance, otherwise I believe they would have observed
the neutrality which had been always so carefully maintained
by the European nations in the country of the Ganges, in
spite of all the wars which took place in Europe. Many of
the French from Chandernagore--officers, Company's servants,
and others--had taken refuge at Cossimbazar with M. Law,
who formed there a party which opposed the English in
various ways. The English, however, forced Siraj-ud-daula,
against his true interest and in spite of his promise to
protect us, to abandon us, and to make M. Law leave his
Factory and go to Patna. This imprudent act was the ruin
of the Prince and put the final touch to our misfortunes,
whilst it has made the English masters of Bengal, and has
filled their coffers with wealth.

"I held on at Dacca till the 22nd of June. I was troubled
as little as was possible in such circumstances, owing, I
think, to the gratitude which the English felt for the services
I had rendered them in Dacca the year before. I had all
the more reason to think this was so because, after the
misfortune which befell Chandernagore, they had often
offered to secure to me all my effects and merchandise in
Murshidabad [?]--they were worth a million--provided I
made over to them the French Factory and all that belonged
to the Company, and would myself leave for Pondicherry
in the following October. They said I should not be considered
a prisoner of war, and should not require to be
exchanged.

"These were, no doubt, very good terms, and most
advantageous to me; but should I not have been dishonoured
for ever if I had had a soul so servile and base as to accept
them? I would have been covered with ignominy in my

own eyes, and without doubt in those of all the world. I
therefore thought it my duty to reject them.

"Things were on this footing when, at the beginning
of June, I learned that the English, having got rid of M.
Law, were marching upon Murshidabad with all their forces
to achieve the destruction of a Prince who was already half
ruined by his own timidity and cowardice, and still further
weakened by the factions formed against him by the chief
members of his own family--a Prince detested by every one
for his pride and tyranny, and for a thousand dreadful crimes
with which he had already soiled his reputation though he
was barely twenty-five years old.

"I knew only too well what was preparing against him,
and I was also most eager to find some honourable means of
escape for myself. M. Chevalier's absence troubled me
greatly, and I did not like to leave him behind me. At last
he arrived on the 16th or 17th. I had taken the precaution
to provide myself with a *parwana*, or passport, signed by
Siraj-ud-daula, allowing me to go where I pleased. That
Prince had recalled M. Law to him, but too late, for I felt
certain he could not rejoin him in time to save him or to
check the progress of his enemies. I was in a hurry therefore
to go and help to save him if that were possible, taking
care, however, to choose a route by which I could escape if,
as I thought probable, he should have succumbed beforehand
to the efforts of the English, and the treason of his subjects.

"It was then the 22nd of June when I started with
about 35 boats,[129] MM. Chevalier, Brayer [possibly a relation
of the M. Brayer who commanded at Patna], Gourlade, the
surgeon, and an Augustine Father, Chaplain of the Factory,

8 European soldiers, of whom several were old and past
service, 17 topass gunners, 4 or 5 of the Company's servants,
and about 25 or 30 peons.[130] There, my dear wife, is the
troop with which thou seest me start upon my adventures.[131]
To these, however, should be added my Christian clerks, my
domestics, and even my cook, all of whom I dressed and
armed as soldiers to assist me in what I expected to be a
losing game, and which, in fact, had results the most disastrous
in the world for my personal interests.

"It was not till seven or eight days after I had set out
with this fine troop that I learned there had been a battle at
Plassey between the English and the Nawab, in which the
latter had been defeated and forced to flee, and that Jafar
Ali Khan, his maternal uncle,[132] had been enthroned in his
place. This report, though likely enough as far as I could
judge, did not come from a source so trustworthy that I could
rely on it with entire faith. Accordingly I did not yet
abandon the route which I had proposed to myself; in fact,
I followed it for some days more, and almost as far as the
mouth of the Patna River.[133] There I learned, beyond possibility
of doubt, that Siraj-ud-daula had been captured, conducted
to Murshidabad, and there massacred; that he had
just missed being rejoined by M. Law, who was coming to
meet him, and could easily have done so if he had followed
the instructions given him and had been willing to march
only three hours longer; and that the English had sent a
body of troops towards Patna to capture or destroy M. Law
if possible."

We have seen in a previous chapter the real reasons why Law was
unable to rejoin Siraj-ud-daula in time for the battle.

"I now saw that a junction with him had become impossible,
unless I determined to run the most evident risk of
losing my liberty and all I had."

It appears that Courtin had the Company's effects, as well as his
own private property and that of his companions, on board his little
fleet.

"This made me change my route immediately. The
mountains of Tibet[134] appeared to me a safe and eminently
suitable asylum until the arrival in the Ganges of the forces
which we flattered ourselves were coming. I therefore directed
my route in this direction, but found myself suddenly and
unexpectedly so close to Murshidabad that for two days
together we heard the sound of the guns fired in honour of
the revolution which had taken place. It is easy to judge
into what alarm this unexpected and disagreeable proximity
threw me. However, we arrived safely, on the 10th of July,
at the capital of the Raja of Dinajpur, who wished to oppose
our passage."

This was the Raja Ram Nath, whom Orme describes as "a Raja, who with
much timidity, was a good man."

"We made it in spite of him, threatening to attack him
if he showed any further intention of opposing us. I do not
know what would have happened if he had had a little firmness,
for we learned afterwards that he had always in his
service a body of 5000 infantry and cavalry. The persons
whom he sent to us had at first suggested that I should pretend
I was English, assuring me that by that means all difficulties
would be removed; but I thought this trick too much
beneath a man of honour for me to make use of it, and, in

fact, I objected to pass for anything but what I really was.

"I found here a French soldier, who had been at the
battle of Plassey, where the brave Sinfray,[135] at the head of
38 Frenchmen, had fought like a hero for a long time, and
had retreated only at the order of Siraj-ud-daula, who, seeing
himself betrayed and the battle lost, sent him word to cease
fighting. This worthy gentleman afterwards took refuge in
Birbhum, the Raja of which country betrayed him, and disgracefully
handed him over to the English in October last."

Courtin is somewhat unfair to the Raja (apparently a Muhammadan, as
he was called Assaduzama Muhammad),[136] for this Prince was an ally
of the English, and had offered Clive the assistance of his forces
before the battle of Plassey. It could be no treachery on his part
to pick up fugitives from the battle, like Sinfray, and hand them
over to his allies. I may as well quote one of the Raja's letters to
Clive, received 28th October, 1757:--

"Before your letter arrived the French were going
through, some woods in my country. I knew they were your
enemies, therefore I ordered my people to surround them. The
French being afraid, some said they were English, and some
Dutch. In the meantime I received your letter that if I
could apprehend them I should send them to you, therefore
I have sent them. Surajah Dowlat has plundered my
country so much, that there is hardly anything left in it."[137]

Courtin continues:--

"To return to my journey and my adventures. I now
found myself outside of Bengal and in sight of the mountains
of Tibet, a month having elapsed since my departure from

Dacca. I was only two or three days distant from these
mountains, and my intention, as thou hast seen above, was to
go there; but I was prevented by the murmurs of my people,
especially the boatmen, who already began to desert in small
parties. Accordingly I accepted an offer made me on the
part of the Raja of Sahibgunj, to give me a site for a fort,
and to aid me with everything I might want. I descended
the river again for a little, and near this site, which was on
the river bank, I commenced a fort, but the thickness of the
forest forced me to abandon it, and I entered a little river
close by, which conducted me to a marsh, on the borders of
which I found an elevated site admirably situated and in a
very agreeable neighbourhood.[138] This belonged to the same
Raja, and with his consent I again set to work, and that
with such promptitude that in less than a month my fortress
commenced to take form, and visibly progressed owing to
the extraordinary efforts I made to complete it. It was
triangular, with a bastion at each angle. At two of the
angles I had found superb trees with very heavy foliage, and
on the third I erected the mast of my boat and hoisted our
flag. All three bastions had four embrasures, a fine entrance
gate opening on the marsh, and a little open turret above,
A small entrance gate led to the open country. The curtains
were carefully pierced for musketry, and strengthened outside
with a trellis work of bamboo, and finished off with banquettes
on the ramparts. An excellent powder magazine
was built in the same way, and, being situated in the interior
of the fort, was quite safe from any accident.

"As I had brought workmen of all kinds with me, the
work went on well, especially as the care of our health made
us all industrious. I was not without cannon, and I mounted
on our ramparts two Swedish guns, which afterwards proved

our safety and preservation.[139] Also being provided with the requisites for making gunpowder, I very soon had nearly 3000 lbs. weight of very good quality.

"Hardly anything remained to complete my fortress, which I had named 'Bourgogne,' except to provide it with a glacis. It was already furnished with a market which was sufficiently flourishing, when to my misfortune I received the false information that our forces, which were said to be considerable, were ready to enter the Ganges, and that there was certain news of the arrival of a very strong squadron at Pondicherry.[140] On the 8th September there broke out at Purneah, and in the province of that name, a Evolution headed by a person named Hazir Ali Khan,[141] who, having seized the capital, at once wrote to me to join him, and assist him against the English and Jafar Ali Khan.[142]

"These two events made me stop everything else and devote myself entirely to getting my boats out of the little river by which I had entered the marsh, and which was now almost quite dried up. I succeeded in doing so after some time, by means of ditches which I cut from the marsh, but this took me more than a month and considerable labour, as I was about two leagues from the great river. To complete my misfortunes, my troop was attacked by sickness, which raged with a violence such as I had scarcely ever seen. It cost me nine soldiers, of whom three were Europeans. The latter were luckily replaced some days after by the same number who joined me.[143] Poor M. Brayer and M. Gourlade had been during almost the whole campaign in the most pitiable condition, especially the former, who I thought a thousand times must have died. As for me, the powders *d'Aillot* preserved me from the pestilential air, and cured

me from the effects of a fall in my ***bajarow***,[144] caused by the
clumsiness of my boatmen. I narrowly escaped breaking
my ribs and back.

"Before quitting Fort Bourgogne I must tell thee, my
dear wife, that I often played there a very grand role. I
was called the 'Fringuey Raja,' or 'King of the Christians.'
I was often chosen as arbiter amongst the little princes in
my neighbourhood, who sent me ambassadors. My reputation
spread so wide, and the respect that I gained was so
great, that the King of Tibet did not disdain to honour me
with an embassy of nearly eight hundred persons, whom I
entertained for nine whole days, and whose chiefs I dismissed
with presents suitable to their rank, their king, our
nation, and the idea which I wished to leave behind me in
this country of the European name. The presents which
were made me consisted of five horses, some bags of scent,
three or four pieces of china, pieces of gilt paper, and a sabre
like those used by the Bhutiyas, or people of Tibet, who are
men as strong and robust as those of Bengal are feeble.
Though pagans like the latter, they eat all kinds of things,
and live almost like the Tartars, from whom they are descended.
They have no beards, and are clothed in a fashion
which is good enough, but which looks singular. They are
very dirty. The complexion of those whom I saw was very
dark, but I know it is not the same in the interior of the
country and in the mountains, where all are as fair as the
Chinese, who are said to be their neighbours. I took some
trouble to form an alliance and to make a party amongst
them. They appeared very willing, but I soon had occasion
to convince myself that not only were they not fitting persons
for my designs, but also that they were playing with me.
It is not that they do not make raids upon the lower country,

but they make these only in the cold weather, always withdrawing
at the commencement of the hot, without trying to
make any permanent conquests.

"There, then, my reign is finished, or nearly so, for the
good news that I continued to receive (though always without
foundation, as I learned afterwards), joined to the entreaties
of Hazir All Khan and to the unhealthy air which continued
to decimate my poor little troop, induced me at last to
abandon my fort, to embark again upon my boats, and to
reapproach Bengal, from which I had hitherto been travelling
away. The second day after my departure was marked by
a very annoying accident, namely the loss of one of my
largest boats, on which was my library and a quantity of my
effects. These were quickly drawn out of the water, but
were none the less ruined for the Company and for me.
From that moment commence my misfortunes. The sixth
day--I had passed three in the salvage of the effects on my
boat--I received a ***pattamar*** (messenger), who informed me
that the English and the troops of Jafar Ali Khan were at
Purneah, from which they had chased Hazir Ali Khan and
wholly destroyed his faction."

From Broome we see that this was in the middle of December, 1757. It
was now that Clive first heard what Courtin was attempting. He
immediately sent orders direct, and also through the Nawab, to Kasim
Ali Khan, Faujdar of Rungpore, and to Raja Ram Nath of Dinajpur, to
seize the French.

"It was almost impossible for me to reascend the river
because of the dry banks and the strong currents which
would have put my boats in danger. However, I found
myself in the country of Rungpore, which was a dependency

of Bengal. I determined nevertheless to remain where I was, flattering myself the English would not come to look for me, nor the Nawab or the ruler of the province think of disturbing themselves about me, as I was doing no harm in the country, and as I was very strict in observing proper order and discipline. I was so confident on this latter head that I did not think of throwing up now entrenchments, and occupied myself only with hunting and walking whilst I awaited the arrival of the French forces. However, one day, towards the middle of January, a secret rumour came to me that Kasim Ali Khan, Faujdar of Rungpore, was coming to attack me. I sent out scouts, who reported that all was tranquil in his town, and that, far from wishing to come and look for a quarrel, he was in fear lest I should march against his town, which was three days' journey from where I was. Doubtless my men deceived me or did not take the trouble to go to Rungpore, for on the 15th of the same month, at 3 p.m., on the opposite side of the river to that on which we were, there appeared a body of soldiers, cavalry and infantry, about 600 in number, who approached so near my fleet that I no longer doubted the correctness of the first advice which had been given me. I ordered a discharge of three guns on this troop, which was so well directed that the enemy were forced to take themselves off and to encamp a little further from me. Next day the commander sent me a present of some fruit, and an intimation that he only wished to see me quit his country. He knew I could not do this without risk, and, according to the custom of the infidels, he gave me the strongest possible assurances of my safety and tranquillity. I took care not to trust to them; I was then, as I said above, without entrenchments and without defence, so in the evening I set to work at surrounding myself with a ditch, the mud taken out of which would

serve me for embrasures. I was short of provisions, which
made me very anxious, and I was still more so when
I learned that the enemy were trying to cut me off from
provisions on all sides, and that their intention was to
capture me by famine or treachery. Their number quickly
increased to 3000 men, of whom a part came over to my
side of the river, and harassed my people whenever they
went out for provisions. This forced me to detach. MM.
Chevalier and Gourlade, with about 10 men, some peons
and boatmen, against one of their little camps, where there
were about 150 men, foot and horse. Our men received
their fire, stormed the camp, and destroyed it after having
put every one to flight. There was not a single person
wounded on our side. This little advantage gave me time to
make a good provision of rice and other things in the villages
near my entrenchments. I cleared out these villages and
drove out the inhabitants, but I was still in need of a
quantity of things necessary to life. To procure these, I
tried to frighten the enemy by cannonading their chief camp
on the other side of the river. This only resulted in making
them withdraw altogether beyond the reach of my guns, not
with the idea of going away, but of starving me out, and, as
I learned later, to give time for a reinforcement of artillery
which they were expecting to arrive. They had already 4
or 5 guns, but their calibre was small compared with mine,
as I was able to see from the balls which fell in my camp
when it was entrenched only on the land side.

"The 19th of January, early in the morning, I sent across
the river a number of workmen, supported by a little detachment
under M. Gourlade, to cut down a grove of bamboos
which masked my guns, and to burn down some houses which
were also in their way. I forbade them to engage the enemy,

and all went well until some topasses and peons advanced
too far towards the enemy's camp, and I heard discharges
so loud and frequent on both sides, that I ordered a retreat
to be beaten in my entrenchments, to make my people recross
the river. I fired my guns continually to facilitate this and to
cover the movement. In this skirmish I had only one soldier
wounded, and I do not know whether the enemy had any
losses. This day more than 1500 shots were fired on both
sides. Some of the guns which the enemy brought up
troubled us greatly, as we were not entrenched on the water
side. Several balls fell at my side or passed over my head.
This determined me to set all my people at work the next
night with torches, to put us under cover on this side
also."

[It was apparently this fight which Kasim Ali reported to Clive on
the 24th of January:--

"I wrote expressly to my people to go and take them"
(the French) "and they went immediately and found them
ready to fight. On both sides there were cannon and
jenjalls.[145] A *nulla*[146] was between them, which the French
crost, and advancing upon my people, fought with great
intrepidity: but luckily, three or four of them being killed,
they retired into their fort."[147]]

"The Moors saw, from my manoeuvre, how important it
was for them to seize the ground which I had intended to
clear, and, contrary to my expectation, established themselves
on it the same evening without my being able to hinder
them, keeping themselves always well hidden behind the
bamboos, where they had nothing to fear from my artillery,
and still less from my musketry. Like me they worked at

night, and, having as many prisoners or other workmen at their command as they wanted, I saw, with regret, next morning the progress which they had made opposite me. I could not dislodge them without risking everything. Weak as I was, I thought it wiser not to hazard anything more in sorties, but to hold myself always on the defensive.

"Sheikh Faiz Ulla (that was the name of the Moorish general) sent me one of his men next day with a present and proposals of peace, the first condition of which was, of course, that I should quit his country, and as, since the dry weather had set in, a very large and dangerous bank had formed in the river seven or eight leagues below me, he offered me one or two thousand workmen to assist in making a passage for my boats. The shocking treachery used by the Moors being well known to me, I refused to accept his offers except on his furnishing me with hostages for his good faith. He first proposed himself, but with such a strong escort that it was not difficult to see that it was a trap which he was setting for me, so as to seize and massacre us. After many debates between our emissaries, he consented to come to my ***bajarow***, he and his servants, and that all of them should serve as hostages until I was quite out of the domains of his master.

"I loyally agreed to this arrangement and made preparations in consequence, but at 7 in the morning on the 23rd of January, the day I expected the hostages, I was awakened by a cannon-shot quickly followed by a second, the ball of which pierced the ***rezai***[148] at the foot of my bed from side to side, and made a great noise. For a long time I had been accustomed to sleep fully dressed, so I was able to go out quickly and give orders in the entrenchments. The treachery and perfidy of the enemy were too manifest; nevertheless, I forbade a single shot to be fired with musket or cannon, and simply recommended my people to be on their guard on the land side. The enemy kept up a continuous and very lively fire until 4 o'clock in the evening. I considered that it would be useless for me to reply, and wished to see how far they would push their insolence. That day we picked up 40 cannon-balls, and our whole loss was one boatman slightly wounded in the leg. From 4 o'clock till night the enemy's fire was continued, but at long intervals. It began again the next morning. I suffered this as on the previous day for a couple of hours, at the end of which. I fired several shots and silenced it. My firing seemed to trouble the enemy more than I expected it would. One of my boats was sunk by a cannon-ball, several were pierced through, and my *rezai*, which used to serve me as a coat, was much damaged.

"The succeeding days passed much in the same manner until the 3rd of February, when, on the same bank and to the north above my fleet, I saw a new entrenchment, which had been thrown up during the preceding night. Its batteries enfiladed mine along their whole length. It was necessary either to risk everything by making a sortie in order to destroy it, or to arrange terms. I determined on the latter, which appeared to me all the more necessary, as I was beginning to be in want of everything, and as I had just received letters which deprived me of all hope of the arrival of our forces in Bengal until April or May. I therefore informed Sheikh Faiz Ulla that I was ready to enter upon negotiations, and the same day he sent me some of his people, with whom I agreed to leave my entrenchments and go down the river. I consented to do this without hostages, but, that it might be done in security, I promised them a sum of money for themselves as well as for their general. This arrangement being agreed to by Sheikh Faiz Ulla, he sent me word that, in order that he might not appear to betray his master, it would be necessary for me next morning to open the fiercest fire possible on his camp; that he would reply; that on both sides it should be with the intention of doing as little hurt as possible; that I should pretend it was to force him to give me a passport, which he would send me in the evening; and that I should then send him the money I had promised. All these precautions were only to assist his rascality, and they appeared to me all the more surprising, as he had already repeatedly informed me that he had his master's permission to give me a passport, and to let me go where I pleased. But of what are these Moors not capable? Without being blind to the continuance of his perfidy, I flattered myself that it might happen that he would not trouble me on my march when he had received my money.

"However this might be, my cannon fired from 10 in the morning till 3 in the evening. Our people, perceiving that the enemy were firing in earnest, did not spare them any more than they spared us, and that which was at first, on our side, only a pretence, finally became serious. At 4 o'clock I received an envoy, who brought me the passport, and to whom I paid the money. He assured me that I might embark my artillery the next morning, and set out the day after without the slightest apprehension of being interfered with, I took my precautions, and, in fear of treachery, kept on shore my two Swedish guns. At last, at seven in the morning, my boats started, having on board only the sick and helpless, and I set out by land with my two guns and the rest of my troop, at the head of which I put myself."

This triumph of time and treachery was reported by Sheikh Faiz Ulla's master, Kasim Ali, to Clive, on the 14th of February:[149]--

"I before wrote you that I had sent forces to fight the French, that they had a fort and strong intrenchments, and that we had a battle with them.... ever since I wrote you last we have been fighting, my people have behaved well, and I make no doubt but you have heard it from other people. God knows what pains and trouble I have taken in this affair. The French being shut up in their fort and undergoing much fatigue by always fighting, and likewise being in want of provisions were obliged to run away in their boats by night, and went towards the Dinajpur country.

My people being always ready to fight followed them.... They can go no other way but through the Dinajpur country. I have therefore wrote expressly to the Rajah to stop the passage."

About this time, though Courtin does not mention it till later, he began to see what the inevitable end must be. He could not cut his way through to join Law, and with the whole country in arms against him he was too weak to hold out for any length of time. Accordingly he sent messengers secretly to Mr. Luke Scrafton, at Murshidabad. It was Scrafton, as I have said above, who wrote to Courtin for assistance when the Nawab of Dacca wanted to take their Factory and imprison the English. Courtin now wrote to him to save him from falling into the hands of the natives, and, on the 18th of February, Scrafton wrote to the Select Committee at Calcutta for the necessary permission.[150]

We now rejoin Courtin:--

"What was my surprise, at the end of an hour and a
half, to see that we were followed by a body of four or five
hundred men, with two guns drawn by oxen. I pretended
not to notice, and continued my march, but at 3 o'clock
in the afternoon, seeing this troop approach, within range of
my pieces, I pointed them at the Moors, and put my force
in a position of defence. Their rascality followed its usual
course, and they sent me word that I had nothing to fear,
that they would not march so close to me any more, and
that they followed me only to preserve the peace and to
hinder my people, especially the stragglers, from committing
any disorder. I received this excuse for what it was worth,
and pretended to be content with, it, seeing clearly that they
were looking for an opportunity to surprise and destroy us.

"Several accidents happening to the boats of the rearguard
prevented my troop and myself from rejoining the
main body of the fleet till far on in the night. I found it
anchored in the most disadvantageous position possible, and
in the morning I saw at a distance of one-eighth of a league
the same body of troops, that had followed me the day before,
establishing and settling itself. A moment later I learned
that Sheikh Faiz Ulla was on the opposite bank with his
army and his artillery, that he intended to wait for me in a
narrow place called Choquova,[151] at the foot of which my boats
must pass, and that he was diligently making entrenchments
there. My embarrassment was then extreme. I found
myself surrounded on all sides; I was without any provisions,
destitute of the most necessary articles of life. In
this perplexity I saw only the most cruel alternatives, either
to surrender or to fight to the death so as to perish with our
arms in our hands. The latter appeared to be less dreadful
than the former.

"After repeated consultations, we determined it would
be best to risk the passage of the fleet by Choquova. We
thought that possibly we should find provisions there, and
that certainly the position could not be worse (for defence)
than that in which we then found ourselves. The passage
was carried out in three hours' time without confusion or
disorder, by means of my Swedish guns on the boat which
led the van. What was our delight to find, not only a better
position than that which we had quitted, but one that was
almost completely entrenched by nature, and had villages
full of rice to the right and left of it.

"Next day I collected provisions in abundance, cleared
the country round for a quarter of a league, and did my best
to ameliorate my condition. The enemy were disconcerted by
my boldness. They pretended as usual, in order to deceive
me the more easily, that they were not surprised at my march.
They feared rightly that if I commenced new entrenchments
all their trouble would begin again. Besides, I had completely
protected myself from the possibility of surprise. *Pourparlers*
for an accommodation were renewed and lasted three
days, at the end of which it was agreed that I should
continue my march, that two hostages should be given me
for my safety, and that the army with its guns should retire
from Choquova, and should be sent a long way ahead across
country, and as, at half a league from this place, the river
was no longer navigable because of the bank which had
formed in it, I should be supplied with people to facilitate
my passage. Thou wilt notice, my dear wife, that in all the
negotiations I had for various reasons and on several occasions
proposed to suspend all hostilities until an answer
could be received from Jafar All Khan and the English, to
whom I said I would write to come to some accommodation

with them, offering to send my letter open. This was repeatedly
refused, but the refusal did not prevent my asking
for the honours of war. My letters were despatched secretly
by my own messengers.

"At last, on the 23rd, I quitted, though with regret
(always expecting treachery), my new position, and approached
the shallow or bank mentioned. It was night when I
arrived. In spite of this I could understand, from the
dreadful noise made by the waters, that I should have
difficulty in traversing this dangerous passage even with the
assistance promised me. I was only too well convinced of
the truth of this when day broke, and I saw that I had
again been betrayed. There was nothing to be seen of the
work which the Moors had engaged to do to lessen the
difficulty of the passage. However, I did not hesitate to
put out with my lighter boats, firmly resolved, if they arrived
safely, to sacrifice the larger, with all that was upon them,
to my safety, and thus to effect my retreat during the night.
With the exception of two, which were lost, they all arrived
safely. During this piece of work, which took up the whole
day, I dissimulated my intentions in the presence of my hostages,
merely letting them see I was somewhat surprised to
find that, contrary to the promise given, there were no workmen,
but that the army, which ought to have been withdrawn,
was still close to us. Their excuses were vague and unsatisfactory.
One of them, who, no doubt, knew the enemy's plans,
asked permission to go to their camp, promising to come
back the next day. Though his demand accorded with my
designs, I agreed to it only after much persuasion, warning
him not to break his *parole* to return the next morning very
early. This he swore to do. As a rule these people think
nothing of an oath. I did not intend to wait for him, which

his comrade clearly perceived, for, seeing that he himself
had been sacrificed by his master's perfidy, he approved of
the resolution I had taken to set out by night, and swore
that he had acted in good faith, and was ignorant of the
treachery that had been concocted. 'You can,' he said to me,
'have my throat cut. You would be justified in doing so;
but I will not quit you, even if you give me permission.
If I went to my own people, they would say that I had
disclosed to you the trick which you have yourself discovered,
and would certainly show me less mercy than I
have experienced from you.' After this I contented myself
with having him closely watched.

"Orders being given to the remaining boats to start by
night, I mounted on horseback to carry certain necessaries
to my detachment on land, which was already a little in
advance and had crossed a small river with the guns. I
had only three blacks with me, and none of us knew the
way. The night was dark, and we wandered from it. I
narrowly escaped being drowned with my horse, and at last
we lost ourselves entirely. If we had been met by any
horsemen, nothing would have been easier than for them to
capture me, our arms and cartridges being all soaked with
water. Luckily I heard our drums beating, and this told us
in what direction we could safely go.

"My intention was to march by land with my troops and
guns. They objected to this, as I was wet to the skin and
had a cold on the chest, which hardly allowed me to speak;
so I went back to the boats, though with much regret, and
resolved to manage so as not to lose sight of my detachment.
I was in constant anxiety about the latter till 8 o'clock the
next day, when we all came together, except one soldier

topass, who, by his own fault, had remained on a big boat which we had abandoned, and a *manjhi*,[152] who was drowned in one of the two little ones which had sunk.

"Finding myself in the territory of the Raja of Dinajpur, I imagined I had nothing to do with any one except him, and that Sheikh Faiz Ulla and his army would not think of following me through a country which, though tributary to the Nawab of Bengal, still in no way belonged to Faiz Ulla's master. The hostage who remained with me, and to whom I spoke about the matter,[153] did not altogether dissuade me from this idea, but counselled me to continue my march and to get farther away, which I did till 6 o'clock in the evening. What was my surprise when, at 9 o'clock, my scouts reported that the enemy were pursuing me, and were not more than a league away at the most. I could not advance during the night for fear of running on the banks or shallows with which the river was filled, and which might cause the loss of my boats and of my people. Accordingly, I did not set out till the morning, and always remained myself in the rear (of the fleet). I had stopped to wait for my land detachment and the guns, and was at some distance from the rest of my little fleet, when, about half-past nine, I heard several musket shots fired. In an instant I was surrounded by the enemy. M. Chevalier, who conducted the land detachment, fortunately perceived my situation, and, seeing my danger, brought up the two guns and fired about 20 shots, which disengaged me, and gave me time to regain my boats by swift rowing. I had with me only Pedro and the Moorish hostage mentioned before. Then I landed with MM. Brayer, Gourlade, and in general every one who was strong enough to defend himself. At the same time I ordered the boats to go on. In this skirmish our loss was only one man slightly wounded in the ear by a musket-ball.

"My little fleet *en route*, we marched by land on the
bank opposite to that on which was, the main body of the
enemy, who had only cavalry, which we did not trouble
ourselves about It was not the same, however, with the
boats. At the end of an hour the boatmen abandoned them
in a sudden panic, and hurried tumultuously to join me.
When my people were collected, I would have tried to go
and recapture my boats, which the enemy had not delayed
to seize; but not only would this have been a rash undertaking
with so small a force against 3000 men, but also
there was a little river which formed an island between my
boats and me, and so prevented the passage of my guns
This determined me to abandon the boats, and to retreat to
Dinajpur, where I hoped to find an asylum with the Raja
whilst I waited for a reply to my letters to Jafar All Khan
and the English. We marched till 1 o'clock in the afternoon
without being harassed or disquieted--no doubt because
during this time Sheikh Faiz Ulla and his people were
occupied in plundering the boats. We were now not very
far from Dinajpur, when we met a body of the Raja's cavalry,
the commander of which begged me to take another road so
as not to pass through his town. Accordingly he gave me
a guide, with whom we marched till half-past five, when we
arrived at a great *gunge* (market place) at the extremity of
Dinajpur. There they lodged us in a great thatched building.
The want of provisions had caused us to suffer very much in
this retreat."

This was the battle of Cantanagar. Kasim Ali described it as follows
to Clive:--

"My people and the French had a battle, and the latter
finding themselves much, beat, they run away, and left their
boats. They went to Oppoor" "and begged protection of
the Kajah's people.... Bahadur Sing came and told my
people to go a little further off, and they would deliver
them up, but they put us off from day to day."[154]

About the time he was writing this, Clive was writing to say that he
had received Courtin's offer of surrender, and that Kasim Ali was to
cease hostilities and allow the French to come to him with their
boats and necessaries. Kasim Ali had received orders to the same
effect from Mr. Scrafton, who informed him he was sending an officer
to accept their surrender. This did not however prevent Kasim Ali
from trying to get hold of them, which accounts for the following
letter from Raja Ram Nath to Clive:[155]--

"The French are now coming from another country by
boats to go towards Muxadavad, and Kasim Ali Khan's
people have followed them, out of his own country into
mine. They have left their boats among Kasim Ali Khan's
people and are now travelling to Jangepors" (? Tangepur).

"When I heard this I sent people with all expedition to look
after them, and I now hear that they have surrounded them.
The French want the Nawab's and your orders and *call for justice*[156]
from you. They have hoisted the Nawab's[157] and
your colours, have put on your cloaths (?) and want to go
to Muxadavad. Kasim Ali Khan's people want to carry
them to Rungpore but they refuse to go, and say that if one
of us is taken they will destroy themselves.[158] I am a poor
Zemindar who pays revenues[159] and ready to obey your
orders. If the Rungpore people should take them by force,
and they should kill themselves, it would be a troublesome

affair."

To return to Courtin's letter.

"The Raja of Dinajpur did not fail to be embarrassed by
the favour which he had shown to us. Fear was the only
motive which influenced him. He sent word to me to
depart by night under an escort of 200 of his people, who
would conduct me to Murshidabad. I was very nearly
accepting his suggestion, but the hunger and thirst, from
which we suffered greatly, prevented me. So I postponed
giving him a final answer till the next morning, and
then, after full reflection, decided not to move from the
place to which. I had been conducted until I received an
answer to the letters sent to Murshidabad. I thought this
all the wiser, as I was informed that nothing would induce
my enemies to approach or attack me in my asylum.[160] The
place was so retired and so well provided with storehouses,
that I found there a greater appearance of security than in
the open country or the escort offered by the Raja, as his
men were subordinate to the same Prince as the people who
composed the army of Sheikh Faiz Ulla, and were likely
enough to abandon me or to join my enemies in overwhelming
me. My conjectures were well founded, as, several days
after, this same Raja, prompted by Sheikh Faiz Ulla, sent
me word that he could not answer for what might happen to
me if I were attacked; that his troops, being subject to
Murshidabad like those of Kasim All Khan, could not
support me, nor fire on the latter. Finally he sent a certain
priest of his faith, a grave man, who came to suggest to us
that our best course was to leave Dinajpur and gain the
open country, otherwise we were lost. He said that he
knew for certain that if I were so obstinate as to persist in

wishing to remain there, orders had been given to attack us,
cut our throats, and send our heads to Murshidabad. This
person wished to terrify us so as to rid the Raja of us, as he
was dying with fright lest war should be made in the very
heart of his town. I replied that I was resolved to defend
myself against any one who attacked me, to set fire to
everything I found within my reach, to kill as many people
as I could, and to die on my guns when I had used up all
my ammunition; that this was also the intention of my companions,
who preferred to die thus, like brave men, rather than
to be exposed to the ignominies and indignities that we should
undergo if we allowed ourselves to be made prisoners by the
people of Kasim All Khan. The timid Raja, threatened by
both parties, found himself in the utmost embarrassment, for
Sheikh Faiz Ulla, at the gates of his town, put, as it were,
his country under contribution, and demanded from him,
with all imaginable insolence, that he should deliver us up
to him, a thing which the Raja found difficult to do.

"Some days passed in this way, during which we had
frequent alarms, but the letters I received from Murshidabad
filled every one with perplexity. The English sent me
people on their own account. One of my private friends,[161]
whom I had been so fortunate as to oblige on a similar
occasion, wrote me not to trouble myself about my boats or
my effects, but to come at once to him, and he would see
that they restored or paid for my property, and that they
gave me all that I might need. The orders received by
Sheikh Faiz Ulla and the Raja at the same time, ordered the
one to leave me in peace and the other to furnish me with
everything I wanted. This put my mind in a condition of
serenity to which it had long been a stranger, and threw my
enemies into much confusion. They proposed that I should

resume possession of my boats. I knew, with absolute certainty, that they had been half looted, still I accepted them on condition they were brought to Dinajpur. They did not wish, to do this; but next morning after reflection they consented, when, in my turn, I declined, and asked only for provisions and other things necessary for my journey. This they had the harshness to refuse, doubtless because they thought that I, being destitute of everything, would have to go down by whatever route they pleased. I would not trust them in anything, fearing treachery.

"At last, without linen, without clothes, except what we had on our bodies, on the 1st of March, the seventeenth day after our retreat[162] we set out with our arms and our two Swedish guns to go to Murshidabad to the English, from whom I had demanded the honours of war."

We learn from the correspondence between Mr. Scrafton and Clive, that Drake, the cowardly Governor of Calcutta, very naturally could not understand what was meant by this claim to the honours of war.[163]

"My guns were conducted by land by a small detachment, the command of which I gave to M. Chevalier, and we embarked on some small boats belonging to the Raja, in which we had hardly room to move.

"I was not yet at the end of my troubles, for on the 3rd of March, after dinner, as I was getting back into my boat, one of the boatmen, wishing to put down a gun, managed to let it off, and sent a bullet through my left shoulder. It passed through the clavicle between the sinew and the bone. Luckily the blow was broken by a button which the bullet first struck; still it passed almost completely through the shoulder and lodged under the skin, which had to be opened behind the shoulder to extract it and also the wad. However unfortunate this wound was, I ought to be very thankful to God that it was so safely directed, and for the further good fortune of finding with one of my people sufficient ointment for the surgeon, who was quite destitute of all necessaries, to dress my shoulder until the ninth day after, when we arrived at Murshidabad.[164] This wound caused me much suffering for the first few days, but, thanks to the Lord, in thirty-two or thirty-three days it was quite healed and without any bad effects.

"We rested ourselves from our fatigue till the 20th at my friend's house, when, with his concurrence and in response to their offers, I went to the Dutch gentlemen at Cossimbazar, where M. Vernet, their chief and an old friend of mine, received us with the greatest kindness. It is from their Settlement that I write to thee, my dear wife. Until the ships sail for England I shall continue to write daily, and tell thee everything that is of interest.[165]

"August 10, 1758.

"My dear wife, I resume my narrative to tell thee that my boats have been restored by the English, as well as all the goods that had not been plundered by Sheikh Faiz Ulla and his people, except the munitions of war. Still, so much of the merchandise, goods and silver, has disappeared that I am ruined for ever, unless the English, who have promised to cause everything to be restored, are able to make the Moors give them up. The English have at length decided on our fate in a way altogether honourable to us. We are not prisoners of war, and so we are not subject to exchange; but we are bound by certain conditions, which they think necessary to their security, and which only do me honour. What has flattered me even more is that the two Swedish guns which I had with me on my campaign have actually been given to me as a present by the commander of the English troops, who is also Governor of Calcutta, with the most complimentary expressions."

Courtin had written to Clive, asking permission to go down to Pondicherry. Clive replied on the 15th of July, 1758, granting permission. His letter concludes:--

"I am at this moment sending an order to the Captain Commandant of our troops to restore to you your two guns. I am charmed at this opportunity of showing you my appreciation of the way in which you have always behaved to the English, and my own regard for your merit."[166]

Courtin continues:--

"Saved from so many perils and sufficiently fortunate to have won such sensible marks of distinction from our enemies, ought not this, my dear wife, to make me hope that the gentlemen of the French Company will do their utmost to procure me some military honour, in order to prove to the English that my nation is as ready as theirs to recognize my services?[167]

"Now, my dear wife, I must end this letter so that it may be ready for despatch. For fear of its being lost I will send in the packet another letter for thee.

"Do not disquiet thyself regarding my health. Thanks to God I am now actually pretty well. I dare not talk to thee of the possibility of our meeting. Circumstances are not favourable for thee to make another voyage to the Indies. That must depend upon events, thy health, peace, and wishes, which, in spite of my tender longing for thee, will always be my guide.

"If the event of war has not been doubly disastrous to me, thou shouldst have received some small remittances, which I have sent, and of which I have advised thee in duplicate and triplicate. If the decrees of the Lord, after my having endured so many misfortunes and sufferings, have also ordained my death before I am in a position to provide what concerns thee, have I not a right to hope that all my friends will use their influence to induce the Company not to abandon one who will be the widow of two men who have served it well, and with all imaginable disinterestedness?

"For the rest I repeat that, thanks to God, I am fairly well.

"I kiss thee, etc., etc."

One would be glad to be assured that Courtin re-established his fortune. If he is, as I suppose, the Jacques Ignace Courtin, who was afterwards *Conseiller au Conseil des Indes*, we may be satisfied he did so; but French East India Company Records are a hopeless chaos at the present moment, and all that one can extract from the English Records is evidence of still further suffering.

From Murshidabad or Cossimbazar, Courtin went down to Chandernagore, whence the majority of the French inhabitants had already been sent to the Madras Coast. The Fort had been blown up, and the private houses were under sentence of destruction, for the English had determined to destroy the town, partly in revenge for the behaviour of Lally, who, acting under instructions from the French East India Company, had shown great severity to the English in Southern India, partly because they did not think themselves strong enough to

garrison Chandernagore as well as Calcutta, and feared the Moors
would occupy it if they did not place troops there, and partly
because they dreaded its restoration to France--which actually
happened--when peace was made. At any rate Courtin found the
remnants of his countrymen in despair, and in 1759 he wrote a
letter[168] to Clive and the Council of Calcutta, from which I
quote one or two paragraphs:--

"With the most bitter grief I have received advice of
the sentence you have passed on the French Settlement
at Chandernagore, by which all the buildings, as well of
the Company as of private persons, are to be utterly
demolished.

"Humane and compassionate as you are, Sirs, you would
be sensibly affected--were your eyes witnesses to it as mine
have been--by the distress to which this order has reduced
the hearts of those unhappy inhabitants who remain in that
unfortunate place, particularly if you knew that there is
nothing left to the majority of them beyond these houses, on
whose destruction you have resolved. If I may believe
what I hear, the motive which incites you is that of reprisal
for what has happened at Cuddalore and Madras: it does
not become me to criticize either the conduct of M. Lally,
our general, who, by all accounts, is a man very much to be
respected by me, or your reasons, which you suppose sufficient.
Granting the latter to be so, permit me, Sirs, to
address myself to your generosity and humanity, and those
admirable qualities, so universally esteemed by mankind,
will encourage me to take the liberty to make certain representations.

"All upbraidings are odious, and nothing is more just
than the French proverb which says, to remind a person of

favours done him cancels the obligation. God forbid, Sirs,
I should be guilty of this to you or your nation by reminding
you for a moment, that these houses, now condemned by
you, served you as an asylum in 1756, and that the owners,
whom you are now reducing to the greatest distress and are
plunging into despair, assisted you to the utmost of their
power, and alleviated your misfortunes as much as they were
able. But what am I saying? Your nation is too polished to
need reminding of what is just. Therefore excuse my saying
that this reason alone is sufficient to cancel the law of
retaliation which you have resolved to execute, and to make
you revoke an order which, I am sure, you could not have
given without much uneasiness of mind. I cast myself at
your feet, imploring, with the most ardent prayers, that
compassion, which I flatter myself I perceive in your hearts,
for these poor creatures, whom you cannot without remorse
render miserable. If you really, Sirs, think I too have had
the happiness to be of some use to you and your nation,
whilst Chief at Dacca, and that I have rendered you some
services, I only beg that you would recollect them for one
moment, and let them induce you to grant the favour I
request for my poor countrymen. I shall then regard it as
the most happy incident in my life, and shall think myself
ten thousand times more indebted to you.

"If, Sirs, you have absolutely imperative reasons for
reprisal, change, if you please, the object of them. I offer
myself a willing victim, if there must be one, and, if blood
were necessary, I should think myself too happy to offer
mine a sacrifice. But as these barbarous methods are not
made use of in nations so civilized as ours, I have one last
offer to make, which is to ransom and buy all the private
houses at Chandernagore, for which I will enter into whatever

engagements you please, and will give you the best
security in my power."

The last words seem to imply that Courtin had recovered his
property, at least to a great extent; but his pathetic appeal was
useless in face of national necessities, and so far was
Chandernagore desolated that, in November of the same year, we read
that the English army, under Colonel Forde, was ambushed by the
Dutch garrison of Chinsurah "amongst the buildings and ruins of
Chandernagore."

From Chandernagore Courtin went to Pondicherry, where he became a
member of the Superior Council. He was one of the chiefs of the
faction opposed to Lally, who contemptuously mentions a printed
"Memorial" of his adventures which Courtin prepared, probably for
presentation to the Directors of the French East India Company.[169]
When, in January, 1761, Lally determined to capitulate, Courtin was
sent to the English commander on the part of the Council. Still
later we find his name attached to a petition, dated August 3, 1762,
presented to the King against Lally.[170] This shows that Courtin
had arrived in France, so that his elevation to the Council of the
Company is by no means improbable.

To any one who has lived long in India it seems unnatural that in
old days the small colonies of Europeans settled there should have
been incited to mutual conflict and mutual ruin, owing to quarrels
which originated in far-off Europe, and which were decided without
any reference to the wishes or interests of Europeans living in the
colonies. The British Settlements alone have successfully survived
the struggle. The least we can do is to acknowledge the merits,
whilst we commiserate the sufferings, of those other gallant men who
strove their best to win the great prize for their own countrymen.
Of the French especially it would appear that their writers have

noticed only those like Dupleix, Bussy, and Lally, who commanded armies in glorious campaigns that somehow always ended to the advantage of the British, and have utterly forgotten the civilians who really kept the game going, and who would have been twice as formidable to their enemies if the military had been subordinate to them. The curse of the French East India Company was Militarism, whilst fortunately for the English our greatest military hero in India, Lord Clive, was so clear-minded that he could write:--

"I have the liberty of an Englishman so strongly implanted in my nature, that I would have the Civil all in all, in all times and in all places, cases of immediate danger excepted."

How much might have been achieved by men like Renault, Law, and Courtin, if they had had an adequate military force at their disposal! They saw, as clearly as did the English, that Bengal was the heart of India, and they saw the English denude Madras of troops to defend Bengal, whilst they themselves were left by the French commanders in a state of hopeless impotence. On the other hand, owing to the English Company's insistence that military domination should be the exception and not the rule, British civilians and British soldiers have, almost always, worked together harmoniously. It was this union of force which gave us Bengal in the time of which I have been writing, and to the same source of power we owe the gradual building up of the great Empire which now dominates the whole of India.

NOTES:

[122: Probably Portuguese half-castes.]

[123: Matchlock men. Consultations of the Dacca Council, 27th June, 1756. Madras Select Committee Proceedings, 9th November, 1756.]

[124: When Courtin was sent by Count Lally with the proposals for the surrender of Pondicherry he had to take an interpreter with him. *Memoirs of Lally*, p. 105.]

[125: I.e. official order.]

[126: I cannot ascertain where M. Fleurin was at this moment. If at Dacca, then Courtin must have left him behind.]

[127: MSS. Francais, Nouvelles Acquisitions, No. 9361. This is unfortunately only a copy, and the dates are somewhat confused. Where possible I have corrected them.]

[128: Calcapur, the site of the Dutch Factory. See note, p. 64.]

[129: From a map by Rennell of the neighbourhood of Dacca it appears that the French Factory was on the River Bourigunga. There are still several plots of ground in Dacca town belonging to the French. One of them, popularly known as Frashdanga, is situated at the mouth of the old bed of the river which forms an island of the southern portion of the town; but I do not think this is the site of the French Factory, as the latter appears to have been situated to the west of the present Nawab's palace.]

[130: Now used in the sense of messengers or office attendants.]

[131: Orme says (bk. viii. p. 285) that Courtin started with 30 Europeans and 100 sepoys. From Law's "Memoir" we see that M. de Carryon took 20 men to Cossimbazar before Law himself left. This accounts for the smallness of Courtin's force.]

[132: Jafar Ali Khan married the sister of Aliverdi Khan, Siraj-ud-daula's grandfather.]

[133: I think he must mean the mouth of the Murshidabad River.]

[134: Courtin means the lower ranges of the Himalayas, inhabited by the Nepaulese, Bhutiyas, etc. His wanderings therefore were in the districts of Rungpore and Dinajpur.]

[135: Sinfray, Secretary to the Council at Chandernagore, was one of the fugitives who, as mentioned above, joined Law at Cossimbazar.]

[136: Assaduzama Muhammad was nephew to Kamgar Khan, the general of Shah Alam. **Holwell. Memorial to the Select Committee**, 1760.]

[137: Orme MSS. India XI., p. 2859, No. 246.]

[138: Orme says the Fort was on the River Teesta, but Rennell marks it more correctly a little away from the river and about fifteen miles south of Jalpaiguri.]

[139: These guns Courtin calls "pieces a la minute." The

proper name should be "canon a la suedoise" or "canon a la minute." They were invented by the Swedes, who used 3-pounders with improved methods for loading and firing, so as to be able to fire as many as ten shots in a minute. The French adopted a 4-pounder gun of this kind in 1743. The above information was given me by Lieut.-Colonel Ottley Perry, on the authority of Colonel Colin, an artillery officer on the French Headquarters Staff.]

[140: This squadron, under the command of Mons. Bouvet, actually did arrive.]

[141: This rebellion was really conducted by Ukil Singh, the Hindoo **Diwan** of Hazir Ali.]

[142: Mir Jafar, Jafar Ali, Mir Jafar Ali Khan, are all variations of the name of the Nawab whom the English placed on the throne after the death of Siraj-ud-daula.]

[143: Law says that the French soldiers who wandered the country in this way were accustomed to disguise themselves as natives and even as Brahmins, when they wished to avoid notice.]

[144: A kind of native house-boat.]

[145: A heavy gun fired from a rest or stand.]

[146: A ditch or ravine.]

[147: Orme MSS. India XI., p. 2901, No. 374.]

[148: A thick quilt used as a covering when in bed, or sometimes like a blanket to wrap oneself in.]

[149: Orme MSS. India XL, p. 2915, No. 417.]

[150: Bengal Select Com. Consultations, 22nd February, 1758.]

[151: I have not been able to identify this place.]

[152: A boatman.]

[153: See note, p. 88.]

[154: Orme MSS. India XI., p. 2923, No. 432.]

[155: Orme MSS. India XL, p. 2926, No. 438.]

[156: This expression is characteristically Indian, and is used when any one, finding himself oppressed, appeals to some great personage for protection.]

[157: The Nawab's flag was the usual Turkish crescent.]

[158: Another Indian expression. The last resource against oppression or injustice in India is to commit suicide by starvation or some violent means, and to lay the blame on the oppressor. This is supposed to bring the curse of murder upon him.]

[159: This means simply that the Raja was not an independent ruler. The sovereign owning all land, *land revenue* and *rent* meant the same thing.]

[160: This seems to want explanation. Probably Courtin had got into some sort of house used for religious ceremonies, such as are often found in or close to the market-places of great landowners.]

[161: He probably refers to Mr. Luke Scrafton.]

[162: I.e. from his entrenchments.]

[163: "Courtin and his party arrived here the 10th. They are 6 soldiers, Dutch, German and Swede, such as took service with the French when our Factory at Dacca fell into the hands of Surajeh Dowleit, 4 gentlemen, some Chitagon (*sic*) fellows and about 20 peons. Courtin, on his way hither, has, by mischance, received a ball through his shoulder. They demanded **honneurs de la guerre**, which Drake has not understood" (**Scrafton to Clive, March** 12, 1758).]

[164: According to Orme, Courtin's force was reduct from 30 to 11 Europeans, and from 100 to 30 sepoys.]

[165: The manuscript I translate from contains only the postscript of the 10th of August.]

[166: A translation. Clive generally wrote to French officers in their own language.]

[167: Such honours were not uncommonly granted. Law was made a Colonel, so was another French partisan named Madec. On the other hand, when a French gentleman had the choice, he often put his elder son in the Company's service and the younger in the army. Law's younger brother was in the army. Renault's elder son was in the Company and the younger in the army.]

[168: Appended to "Bengal Public Proceedings," May 31, 1759.]

[169: I do not know whether this "Memorial" still exists, but see "Memoirs of Count Lally," p. 53.]

[170: "Memoirs of Count Lally," p. 367.]

The Codes Of Hammurabi And Moses
W. W. Davies

QTY

The discovery of the Hammurabi Code is one of the greatest achievements of archaeology, and is of paramount interest, not only to the student of the Bible, but also to all those interested in ancient history...

Religion   **ISBN:** *1-59462-338-4*   **Pages:**132

MSRP $12.95

The Theory of Moral Sentiments
Adam Smith

QTY

This work from 1749. contains original theories of conscience amd moral judgment and it is the foundation for systemof morals.

Philosophy **ISBN:** *1-59462-777-0*   **Pages:**536

MSRP $19.95

Jessica's First Prayer
Hesba Stretton

QTY

In a screened and secluded corner of one of the many railway-bridges which span the streets of London there could be seen a few years ago, from five o'clock every morning until half past eight, a tidily set-out coffee-stall, consisting of a trestle and board, upon which stood two large tin cans, with a small fire of charcoal burning under each so as to keep the coffee boiling during the early hours of the morning when the work-people were thronging into the city on their way to their daily toil...

Pages:84

Childrens   **ISBN:** *1-59462-373-2*   *MSRP $9.95*

My Life and Work
Henry Ford

QTY

Henry Ford revolutionized the world with his implementation of mass production for the Model T automobile. Gain valuable business insight into his life and work with his own auto-biography... "We have only started on our development of our country we have not as yet, with all our talk of wonderful progress, done more than scratch the surface. The progress has been wonderful enough but..."

Pages:300

Biographies/   **ISBN:** *1-59462-198-5*   *MSRP $21.95*

The Art of Cross-Examination
Francis Wellman

QTY

I presume it is the experience of every author, after his first book is published upon an important subject, to be almost overwhelmed with a wealth of ideas and illustrations which could readily have been included in his book, and which to his own mind, at least, seem to make a second edition inevitable. Such certainly was the case with me; and when the first edition had reached its sixth impression in five months, I rejoiced to learn that it seemed to my publishers that the book had met with a sufficiently favorable reception to justify a second and considerably enlarged edition. ..

Pages:412

Reference   ISBN: *1-59462-647-2*   *MSRP $19.95*

On the Duty of Civil Disobedience
Henry David Thoreau

QTY

Thoreau wrote his famous essay, On the Duty of Civil Disobedience, as a protest against an unjust but popular war and the immoral but popular institution of slave-owning. He did more than write—he declined to pay his taxes, and was hauled off to gaol in consequence. Who can say how much this refusal of his hastened the end of the war and of slavery ?

Law   ISBN: *1-59462-747-9*   **Pages:48**
                                          MSRP $7.45

Dream Psychology Psychoanalysis for Beginners
Sigmund Freud

QTY

Sigmund Freud, born Sigismund Schlomo Freud (May 6, 1856 - September 23, 1939), was a Jewish-Austrian neurologist and psychiatrist who co-founded the psychoanalytic school of psychology. Freud is best known for his theories of the unconscious mind, especially involving the mechanism of repression; his redefinition of sexual desire as mobile and directed towards a wide variety of objects; and his therapeutic techniques, especially his understanding of transference in the therapeutic relationship and the presumed value of dreams as sources of insight into unconscious desires.

Pages:196

Psychology   ISBN: *1-59462-905-6*   *MSRP $15.45*

The Miracle of Right Thought
Orison Swett Marden

QTY

Believe with all of your heart that you will do what you were made to do. When the mind has once formed the habit of holding cheerful, happy, prosperous pictures, it will not be easy to form the opposite habit. It does not matter how improbable or how far away this realization may see, or how dark the prospects may be, if we visualize them as best we can, as vividly as possible, hold tenaciously to them and vigorously struggle to attain them, they will gradually become actualized, realized in the life. But a desire, a longing without endeavor, a yearning abandoned or held indifferently will vanish without realization.

Pages:360

Self Help   ISBN: *1-59462-644-8*   *MSRP $25.45*

www.bookjungle.com *email: sales@bookjungle.com fax: 630-214-0564 mail: Book Jungle PO Box 2226 Champaign, IL 61825*

QTY

The Rosicrucian Cosmo-Conception Mystic Christianity *by Max Heindel*   ISBN: *1-59462-188-8*   **$38.95**
The Rosicrucian Cosmo-conception is not dogmatic, neither does it appeal to any other authority than the reason of the student. It is: not controversial, but is: sent forth in the, hope that it may help to clear...   *New Age/Religion Pages 646*

Abandonment To Divine Providence *by Jean-Pierre de Caussade*   ISBN: *1-59462-228-0*   **$25.95**
"The Rev. Jean Pierre de Caussade was one of the most remarkable spiritual writers of the Society of Jesus in France in the 18th Century. His death took place at Toulouse in 1751. His works have gone through many editions and have been republished...   *Inspirational/Religion Pages 400*

Mental Chemistry *by Charles Haanel*   ISBN: *1-59462-192-6*   **$23.95**
Mental Chemistry allows the change of material conditions by combining and appropriately utilizing the power of the mind. Much like applied chemistry creates something new and unique out of careful combinations of chemicals the mastery of mental chemistry...   *New Age Pages 354*

The Letters of Robert Browning and Elizabeth Barret Barrett 1845-1846 vol II   ISBN: *1-59462-193-4*   **$35.95**
by Robert Browning and Elizabeth Barrett   *Biographies Pages 596*

Gleanings In Genesis (volume I) *by Arthur W. Pink*   ISBN: *1-59462-130-6*   **$27.45**
Appropriately has Genesis been termed "the seed plot of the Bible" for in it we have, in germ form, almost all of the great doctrines which are afterwards fully developed in the books of Scripture which follow...   *Religion/Inspirational Pages 420*

The Master Key *by L. W. de Laurence*   ISBN: *1-59462-001-6*   **$30.95**
In no branch of human knowledge has there been a more lively increase of the spirit of research during the past few years than in the study of Psychology, Concentration and Mental Discipline. The requests for authentic lessons in Thought Control, Mental Discipline and...   *New Age/Business Pages 422*

The Lesser Key Of Solomon Goetia *by L. W. de Laurence*   ISBN: *1-59462-092-X*   **$9.95**
This translation of the first book of the "Lemegton" which is now for the first time made accessible to students of Talismanic Magic was done, after careful collation and edition, from numerous Ancient Manuscripts in Hebrew, Latin, and French...   *New Age/Occult Pages 92*

Rubaiyat Of Omar Khayyam *by Edward Fitzgerald*   ISBN:*1-59462-332-5*   **$13.95**
Edward Fitzgerald, whom the world has already learned, in spite of his own efforts to remain within the shadow of anonymity, to look upon as one of the rarest poets of the century, was born at Bredfield, in Suffolk, on the 31st of March, 1809. He was the third son of John Purcell...   *Music Pages 172*

Ancient Law *by Henry Maine*   ISBN: *1-59462-128-4*   **$29.95**
The chief object of the following pages is to indicate some of the earliest ideas of mankind, as they are reflected in Ancient Law, and to point out the relation of those ideas to modern thought.   *Religiom/History Pages 452*

Far-Away Stories *by William J. Locke*   ISBN: *1-59462-129-2*   **$19.45**
"Good wine needs no bush, but a collection of mixed vintages does. And this book is just such a collection. Some of the stories I do not want to remain buried for ever in the museum files of dead magazine-numbers an author's not unpardonable vanity..."   *Fiction Pages 272*

Life of David Crockett *by David Crockett*   ISBN: *1-59462-250-7*   **$27.45**
"Colonel David Crockett was one of the most remarkable men of the times in which he lived. Born in humble life, but gifted with a strong will, an indomitable courage, and unremitting perseverance...   *Biographies/New Age Pages 424*

Lip-Reading *by Edward Nitchie*   ISBN: *1-59462-206-X*   **$25.95**
Edward B. Nitchie, founder of the New York School for the Hard of Hearing, now the Nitchie School of Lip-Reading, Inc, wrote "LIP-READING Principles and Practice". The development and perfecting of this meritorious work on lip-reading was an undertaking...   *How-to Pages 400*

A Handbook of Suggestive Therapeutics, Applied Hypnotism, Psychic Science   ISBN: *1-59462-214-0*   **$24.95**
by Henry Munro   *Health/New Age/Health/Self-help Pages 376*

A Doll's House: and Two Other Plays *by Henrik Ibsen*   ISBN: *1-59462-112-8*   **$19.95**
Henrik Ibsen created this classic when in revolutionary 1848 Rome. Introducing some striking concepts in playwriting for the realist genre, this play has been studied the world over.   *Fiction/Classics/Plays 308*

The Light of Asia *by sir Edwin Arnold*   ISBN: *1-59462-204-3*   **$13.95**
In this poetic masterpiece, Edwin Arnold describes the life and teachings of Buddha. The man who was to become known as Buddha to the world was born as Prince Gautama of India but he rejected the worldly riches and abandoned the reigns of power when...   *Religion/History/Biographies Pages 170*

The Complete Works of Guy de Maupassant *by Guy de Maupassant*   ISBN: *1-59462-157-8*   **$16.95**
"For days and days, nights and nights, I had dreamed of that first kiss which was to consecrate our engagement, and I knew not on what spot I should put my lips..."   *Fiction/Classics Pages 240*

The Art of Cross-Examination *by Francis L. Wellman*   ISBN: *1-59462-309-0*   **$26.95**
Written by a renowned trial lawyer, Wellman imparts his experience and uses case studies to explain how to use psychology to extract desired information through questioning.   *How-to/Science/Reference Pages 408*

Answered or Unanswered? *by Louisa Vaughan*   ISBN: *1-59462-248-5*   **$10.95**
Miracles of Faith in China   *Religion Pages 112*

The Edinburgh Lectures on Mental Science (1909) *by Thomas*   ISBN: *1-59462-008-3*   **$11.95**
This book contains the substance of a course of lectures recently given by the writer in the Queen Street Hall, Edinburgh. Its purpose is to indicate the Natural Principles governing the relation between Mental Action and Material Conditions...   *New Age/Psychology Pages 148*

Ayesha *by H. Rider Haggard*   ISBN: *1-59462-301-5*   **$24.95**
Verily and indeed it is the unexpected that happens! Probably if there was one person upon the earth from whom the Editor of this, and of a certain previous history, did not expect to hear again...   *Classics Pages 380*

Ayala's Angel *by Anthony Trollope*   ISBN: *1-59462-352-X*   **$29.95**
The two girls were both pretty, but Lucy who was twenty-one who supposed to be simple and comparatively unattractive, whereas Ayala was credited, as her Bombwhat romantic name might show, with poetic charm and a taste for romance. Ayala when her father died was nineteen...   *Fiction Pages 484*

The American Commonwealth *by James Bryce*   ISBN: *1-59462-286-8*   **$34.45**
An interpretation of American democratic political theory. It examines political mechanics and society from the perspective of Scotsman James Bryce   *Politics Pages 572*

Stories of the Pilgrims *by Margaret P. Pumphrey*   ISBN: *1-59462-116-0*   **$17.95**
This book explores pilgrims religious oppression in England as well as their escape to Holland and eventual crossing to America on the Mayflower, and their early days in New England...   *History Pages 268*

QTY

The Fasting Cure *by Sinclair Upton*   ISBN: *1-59462-222-1*   **$13.95**
*In the Cosmopolitan Magazine for May, 1910, and in the Contemporary Review (London) for April, 1910, I published an article dealing with my experi-
ences in fasting. I have written a great many magazine articles, but never one which attracted so much attention...*   New Age/Self Help/Health Pages 164

Hebrew Astrology *by Sepharial*   ISBN: *1-59462-308-2*   **$13.45**
*In these days of advanced thinking it is a matter of common observation that we have left many of the old landmarks behind and that we are now press ng
forward to greater heights and to a wider horizon than that which represented the mind-content of our progenitors...*   Astrology Pages 144

Thought Vibration or The Law of Attraction in the Thought World   ISBN: *1-59462-127-6*   **$12.95**

by William Walker Atkinson   Psychology/Religion Pages 144

Optimism *by Helen Keller*   ISBN: *1-59462-108-X*   **$15.95**
*Helen Keller was blind, deaf, and mute since 19 months old, yet famously learned how to overcome these handicaps, communicate with the world, and
spread her lectures promoting optimism. An inspiring read for everyone...*   Biographies/Inspirational Pages 84

Sara Crewe *by Frances Burnett*   ISBN: *1-59462-360-0*   **$9.45**
*In the first place, Miss Minchin lived in London. Her home was a large, dull, tall one, in a large, dull square, where all the houses were alike, and all the
sparrows were alike, and where all the door-knockers made the same heavy sound...*   Childrens/Class c Pages 88

The Autobiography of Benjamin Franklin *by Benjamin Franklin*   ISBN: *1-59462-135-7*   **$24.95**
*The Autobiography of Benjamin Franklin has probably been more extensively read than any other American historical work, and no other book of its kind
has had such ups and downs of fortune. Franklin lived for many years in England, where he was agent...*   Biographies/History Pages 332

Name	
Email	
Telephone	
Address	
City, State ZIP	

☐ **Credit Card**   ☐ **Check / Money Order**

Credit Card Number	
Expiration Date	
Signature	

Please Mail to: Book Jungle
PO Box 2226
Champaign, IL 61825
or Fax to: 630-214-0564

ORDERING INFORMATION

web: *www.bookjungle.com*
email: *sales@bookjungle.com*
fax: *630-214-0564*
mail: *Book Jungle PO Box 2226 Champaign, IL 61825*
or PayPal *to sales@bookjungle.com*

Please contact us for bulk discounts

DIRECT-ORDER TERMS

**20% Discount if You Order
Two or More Books**
Free Domestic Shipping!
Accepted: Master Card, Visa,
Discover, American Express

www.ingramcontent.com/pod-product-compliance
Lightning Source LLC
Chambersburg PA
CBHW080908020726
47502CB00008B/2387

9781438595498